MY FOOT'S
IN THE STIRRUP . . .
MY PONY
WON'T STAND

D1443259

G·K
Hall
&C°.

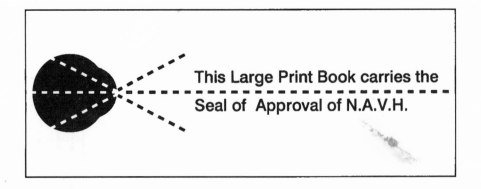

MY FOOT'S IN THE STIRRUP . . . MY PONY WON'T STAND

Stephen Bly

G.K. Hall & Co. • Thorndike, Maine

Copyright © 1996 by Stephen Bly

Published in 1998 by arrangement with Crossway Books.

G.K. Hall Large Print Western Series.

The text of this Large Print edition is unabridged.
Other aspects of the book may vary from the original edition.

Set in 16 pt. Plantin by Al Chase.

Printed in the United States on permanent paper.

Library of Congress Cataloging in Publication Data

Bly, Stephen A., 1944–
    My foot's in the stirrup — my pony won't stand / Stephen Bly.
      p.   cm. — (Code of the West ; bk. 5)
    ISBN 0-7838-0177-7 (lg. print : hc. : alk. paper)
    1. Large type books.   I. Title. II. Series: Bly, Stephen A., 1944–
Code of the West ; bk. 5.
    [PS3552.L93M9 1998]
    813′.54—dc21   98-18672

For
THE WILD BUNCH
At Broken Arrow Crossin'

1

Monday, August 27, 1883, ten miles north of Pine Bluffs, Wyoming Territory.

The bullet that struck Brownie seemed to fall straight out of the sky. When the horse went down, Tap Andrews didn't know whether to dive to the right or to the left.

But either way, he knew he had to come up firing.

He hit the dry Wyoming dirt with as much grace as a tree limb falling to the ground during a windstorm. His ribs slammed into the baked prairie, and he jerked his leg free from under the struggling horse. He squeezed one shot straight up the trail at the blue Wyoming sky, hoping it would buy him time to find protection. Holding his '73 Winchester parallel to his body, Tap rolled a good twenty feet out into the prairie where the buckskin-colored weeds were about a foot and a half tall and supplied a little cover, provided he kept his head down and didn't move a muscle.

The second shot finished off the downed horse. The third ripped into the earth about ten feet from Tap.

They're up the trail, but how can they see me without me seeing them? There's nothing to hide behind until Lodgepole Creek. Where are they?

Another shot rang out — this time far to the

right side of the dead horse. Tap fought back the urge to lift his head to spy out his attackers.

Brownie, you've been a good friend ever since I broke out of ATP at Yuma. I sorely regret your early demise and am hoping to figure out a way not to join you in the very near future. But it would have been more considerate if you had fallen sideways. Then I could have a little protection.

Tap wiggled to extract the rifle from under his body. Holding the twenty-four-inch round-barreled Winchester in the weeds beside him, he raised the upper tang long-range peep sight.

Another bullet tore the dirt halfway between him and Brownie.

Yeah, I know you're up there somewhere. I just don't know who you are or how many. But my guess is, there are three of you, and one of you is riding a mare with a broken right rear shoe. And somewhere on the other side of that roll in the prairie graze about sixty-four head of rebranded rustled cattle.

I'd guess you're about 150 to 200 yards away with a Sharps .50 caliber set up on a rock or shootin' rest. You can hit a horse . . . but can you hit someone who's shootin' back?

Tap loosened the eye cup and cranked the sight up to the hand-filed notch. It was 180 yards — give or take a few.

Once he tightened the eye cup in place, he pulled the hammer off the safety position and slid the dust cover back with his thumb. He spotted the brass cartridge already in the chamber, and his right hand slipped effortlessly into place around the trigger as he continued to lie flat in the grass.

Another shot exploded dirt about five feet to his right.

They're gettin' closer. Just give me one shot . . . if I have room!

A 400-grain lead bullet ripped into the hard clay soil only two feet from where Tap lay in the grass. He didn't have time to worry about the dirt that blasted his hands and face, because the minute he heard the report of the rifle, he raised himself up on one elbow and squeezed the trigger of his rifle aimed two inches below the brim of a distant brown hat.

Tap then tucked the gun to his side and immediately rolled further away from Brownie. Several handgun shots rattled the earth in his general direction, and the man with the brown hat collapsed on the crest of the gentle rolling prairie.

That's one. Lord, I don't even know who I'm shootin' at. If they'd just git up and ride away, it would be fine with me.

The air was so dead still and heavy that his gun smoke still hung in the air in his previous position, attracting shots so widely scattered Tap began to worry about getting hit purely by chance.

He had cocked the lever on the rifle and now waited in the short grass for another opportunity.

They're usin' pistols to flush me out. And savin' the Sharps for when I raise up. You boys do learn, don't ya? Well, I hope that old boy holding the rifle

9

is a pretty good shot, because if he scatters this, I could be in real trouble.

Lying flat on his stomach and still holding the rifle in his right hand, he reached across his back with his left hand and drew his Colt .44 out of the holster. The heat of the earth baked his now hatless head. Sweat puddled up in the dust under his face.

It's 100° and not a cloud in the sky. I might as well be in Arizona.

He drew the rifle to his right side, holding it with his right hand, and cocked the single-action Colt with the left.

Well, if I don't shoot myself, this might work.

Without raising up at all, Tap fired the revolver wildly into the air, leaving a heavy puff of smoke hanging above the weeds. He dropped the gun in the grass and rolled about three feet back in Brownie's direction. As he expected, the big-bore rifle blasted, and a bullet ripped through the soil exactly where the weeds outlining his former position still lay compressed.

But his eyes were focused on a narrow-brimmed black hat hunkered far ahead on the prairie crest.

Tap fired from his one-elbow position again, and then he rolled even closer to Brownie, trying to stay in the thickest part of the weeds. He barely had to time to see the man slump down to the Wyoming soil.

That's two. 'Course, I could be wrong. There could be more than three of 'em.

He wanted to reach back for the dropped Colt, but it was too far away and seemed to be lying on the very spot the remaining gunman was aiming for. Tap cocked the lever-action rifle and tried to sense the man's next move.

If he was smart, he'd slip back there, take all three horses, and ride off. He knows I can't follow him. But it's pride now. He can't back out. A three-to-one ambush is pretty good odds, only you boys picked a lousy place for it. You had to commit yourself at 200 yards. You can't shoot a man in the back that way.

Shots sporadically kicked up dirt around Tap's position as he lay flat on his stomach, cheek down to the dirt. A sharp sting on his left hand caused him to jerk his arm close to his body for inspection.

Ants!

Big red ants!

He brushed them off in the weeds and drew a bullet only five feet in front of him.

Lord, I know they're Your industrious little creatures, but . . . couldn't You keep them some other place?

The shooting stopped. Tap tried to shake the ants off his arm without revealing his position. They seemed to be swarming closer to him.

Andrews, now is the time to do something!

Tap reached down slowly with his left hand and yanked the buckhorn knife out of his boot and eased it beside him in the dirt. Then he tugged off his red bandanna.

Why are the weeds shorter on my right? Why does

it work that way? I'll have to roll over into those blasted ants!

Scooting the knife and the bandanna above his head, he kept his face to the dirt. Then he tied the bandanna to the buckhorn handle and slowly transferred the Winchester to his left hand. With his right hand clutching on the knife, he extended it as far out as he could and then quickly jabbed the knife blade into the hard dirt. As the red bandanna flagged the knife's position, Tap rolled to the left, back into the ants, and up on his elbow.

The bullet from the Sharps shattered the buckhorn handle of the large Bowie knife, but Tap's bullet found its mark. The distant gunman dropped to the Wyoming soil next to his accomplices. The prairie was silent again. Tap waited a moment. Then he raised to his knees, the Winchester still tucked to his shoulder and his finger tight on the trigger. There was absolutely no movement from the gunmen.

Three sharp bites stung his left arm, and one dug into his left side. Tap leaped to his feet.

"Those ants!" he hollered in torment.

He tried brushing them off his arm, slapping them through his rough gray cotton shirt. He could feel sharp stings on his back, his arms, his neck.

After holstering his Colt, he scooted up the hill, trying to keep the rifle pointed the direction of the downed gunmen and open his shirt at the same time. Even the heat of the sun felt cooler on his bare chest than the fiery bites of the swarming red ants.

When he reached the crest of the prairie roll, he found all three men . . . dead. Each one had been shot about two to three inches below the brim of their hats.

"You boys didn't give me nothin' else to aim at," Tap explained. He then gazed to the north at sixty-four head of TS beef that had been crudely rebranded I8I.

Tap dropped the Winchester in the dirt, pulled off his shirt, and let his suspenders hang down the side of his chap-encased britches. He slapped and rubbed his arms, shoulders, back, and chest. Then he shook and snapped his shirt furiously.

With the shirt tossed across his shoulder, he rolled the gunmen over on their backs. "It wasn't worth it, boys. Givin' up your life for rustled cattle — it wasn't a good bargain. You should have gone to work for the railroad or in a coal mine and earned an honest dollar. But you make your choices and live with the results. May God have mercy on your souls. I don't even know your names or if you were workin' on your own or for someone else."

Both legs were suddenly attacked at the same time. Tap slapped his legs and danced across the prairie. The ants had moved lower when he pulled off his shirt. The stinging was so intense that he hardly noticed a large wagon pulled by a team of four mules rattle up the slight draw from the west.

13

Tap buttoned up his britches, pulled the suspenders up on his bare shoulders, and retrieved his Winchester, while clutching his shirt in his left hand. Driving the wagon was a young man in his late teens or early twenties with a round face and easy smile. He wore a tattered bowler and was trying to grow a mustache. He pulled right up to where the three bodies lay scattered on the prairie.

"Saw you dancin' around from a mile back," the young man drawled. "What happened?" He pushed his hat back leaving a dirt line straight across his forehead.

Tap shuddered as he vigorously rubbed his arms. "It's those red demons!" he muttered as he bent over and tried scratching his legs through worn brown leather chaps and tan canvas duckings.

"Red demons? You mean Injuns? You had a run-in with Injuns?"

"No . . . no, ants. They're about to eat me alive."

The young man's blue eyes widened. "You mean to tell me ants killed them three on the ground?"

"Oh, them? No." Tap brushed and scratched at his hair. "I killed them, but I was layin' in a bed of ants."

The man slowly began to reach under the wagon seat.

"Don't try it, son!" Tap swung the rifle toward him.

"You goin' to kill me, too?" the man blurted out.

"Not unless you pull out a gun from under that wagon seat."

"That's fair enough. The gun stays put. What happened here anyway?"

"These three have been rustlin' some of Tom Slaughter's TS beef. I tracked them down this far, and they jumped me."

"Who are they?"

"I don't have any idea."

"You know Slaughter?"

"Yeah, I work for him and several other ranchers. I'm the brand inspector."

"No foolin'? I'd like to see Slaughter about a job myself. Is he still in Pine Bluffs?"

"Yep . . . provided he didn't go into Cheyenne or Denver to do some business."

The man surveyed the prairie with wide, easy eyes. "Anything I can do for you?"

"You got a shovel?"

"Yes, sir, I do."

"I'd like to borrow it, if I might."

"Surely. You goin' to bury these men?"

"Nope. I'm going to bury my horse."

"Your horse? I never heard of a man burying a horse out here on the prairie."

"They killed my horse. He's been a good partner to me. I aim to see that the coyotes and vultures don't pick his bones. It's the least a man can do."

"Well, I'll be."

15

"But I would like for you to take a message and these three hombres into town."

"You want me to haul the bodies in?"

"I'd appreciate it, son. Can you do that for me? I'll load them up for you."

"How about the ponies?"

"I'll round them up and bring them myself. You're pullin' an empty rig, aren't you?" Tap rubbed his dark brown mustache and his chin. His face continued to feel itchy.

"Regretfully so. They're all gone, you know."

"What's all gone?"

"The buffalo. I won this hidin' outfit in a poker game in Custer City and worked my way down from the Black Hills. I didn't find even one shaggy back. They're all gone. Just like they was ghosts. You interested in buyin' a hidin' outfit? I'll sell you ever'thing cheap."

"Not interested, son."

As Tap pushed the third body into the wagon, the young man pulled all three forward and unfolded a canvas over the top of them.

"What about them bovines?" The young man waved his arm at the cattle. His expression seemed to be locked in a permanent smile. "You aren't going to leave them out here for Sioux bait, are ya?"

"I'll gather the ponies and stick with the herd until Tom Slaughter sends some boys out to drive them home. Tell him I'm at the head of Antelope Draw." Tap slipped on his shirt, but he was still rubbing the bites on his arms.

"Here's the shovel, but I don't envy you digging a hole big enough for a horse in this hard dirt. You got a hat, don't ya?"

"Yeah, it's down the slope a ways. Thanks, son, I appreciate your help. If you're still in Pine Bluffs when I get home, I'll buy you supper."

"I'll take you up on that, mister. But I don't reckon I can figure how one man can get ambushed on the open prairie and take out three men."

"Most bushwhackers are only good at shootin' in the back. They seem to lose their enthusiasm when you start tossin' lead back at them."

"What did you say your name was?"

"Tap Andrews."

"Andrews?" The young man stared. "Andrews? Say, you ain't related to that deputy that took on Del Gatto's gang a few months back over at Cheyenne?"

"Yeah, you might say we're related."

"I read about that up in Deadwood. You're him, ain't ya?"

Tap cautiously began to button his shirt. "Yeah, I'm him."

"No kiddin'? So I met the famous Tapadera Andrews."

"I'm afraid it isn't much of an honor."

"Well . . . 'course, it ain't like meetin' Wyatt Earp, Bill Cody, or Stuart Brannon . . . but you sure stirred up some interest in Deadwood. Some of 'em thought the city ought to send down and get you to come be the town marshal, but those who wanted that got shot the next day, and most

17

folks have just let the matter pass."

"Good choice. I've retired from marshalin' — too much shootin'," Tap admitted.

"Too much shootin'? What do you call this? It ain't exactly a Sunday school picnic I'm haulin' in my wagon."

"No, son. You're right about that."

"You know, I'm goin' to make a name for myself someday. It'll be right there in the newspaper with the rest of you famous hombres."

"What is your name, son?" Tap asked.

"Robert Leroy Parker, sir."

"Well, Robert Leroy Parker, you hire on with Tom Slaughter and learn the business. One of these days you'll be some rich Front Range rancher yourself. Why, the *Cheyenne Daily Leader* will probably want you to run for governor."

"No, sir, Mr. Andrews, I don't think I'll go into ranchin'." Parker flashed his wide, easy grin. "Shoot, it's too much work."

"Yeah." Tap shook his head and sighed. "That's exactly what those three in the wagon must have thought. I'll see you in town, young Mr. Parker."

The wagon rolled slowly south raising dust with every creak of the wheels. The young man turned once to call out, "You don't have to call me Mr. Parker. Ever'one just calls me Butch."

Pepper Andrews pulled back a flowered cotton curtain that served as a pantry door and gazed at several airtight jars on the top shelf. They were stacked exactly one inch apart, and each showed traces of fine red dust. The room stretched the full width of the house, but was barely eight feet deep. At one time it had been a covered back porch. Now it served as pantry, sewing room, and bedroom.

Pepper stepped over to the door that swung open to a hard-packed dirt backyard that sloped in the shade of two giant cottonwoods.

"Angelita!" she called.

If she went down to the stockyards again, Tap will be furious. Why is it "I'm going out to the backyard to play" never ever means that she goes out to the backyard to play?

"Angelita!"

Pepper enjoyed a slight movement in the hot summer air. Her shoes felt tight on her feet. She didn't glance down because she knew she couldn't see them anyway. There was a dull throbbing pain in her lower back, and she reached around her apron string and tried to rub the aching spot.

It won't be long before I won't be able to tie my apron at all! Lord, I'm glad Angelita is with us. She has been good company to me. But I would enjoy it more if You'd keep her out of trouble. She has got to be the most ambitious ten-year-old You ever created. Would it be too much to ask if she might settle down a little — real soon?

Pepper closed the door and gave up on the idea of dusting the pantry. Kneading her sore back, she scooted through the small kitchen into the front room of the neatly painted wood-frame house on Amarillo Street.

Pepper studied herself in a mirror hung over a tiny table next to the front door.

Well, Pepper girl, it's still you. The hair's still blonde. The eyes still green. The nose is still a little crooked. The freckles still show. And you still look tired.

But last time . . . last time I didn't show until almost seven months. Last time I was hardly sick a day until those final horrible two weeks. Last time my back didn't ache, my feet didn't swell, and my legs didn't break out in a rash.

Last time . . . Lord, last time I lost the baby.

Pepper brushed back a tear from the corner of her eye and continued to stare into the mirror.

"Well, Pepper Andrews," she muttered, "your husband says you look 'fleshed out' a little. I look fat. I *feel* fat . . . and tired . . . and sore."

Two more months.

Oh, joy.

You know, Lord, if there's some other way to have babies . . . I know. I know, it was my idea. Maybe I could just go to sleep for a long nap and wake up when it's all over.

The front door flung open, almost hitting her. Angelita, dressed in a long off-white, long-sleeved cotton dress, burst into the room with a wide but sheepish grin.

"Guess what happened to me?" she lisped.

"Angelita! How on earth did you lose your tooth?" Pepper gasped.

"Oh, that? It just fell out. Now I can grow a beautiful adult tooth."

"How did the back of your dress get dirty? Did that happen when your tooth fell out?"

"Oh, no. I tripped running home. These long dresses aren't very comfortable for running, you know. They should let girls wear britches."

"Ladies do not *ever* wear britches," Pepper lectured. "Come here and let me see. . . . Is it bleeding?"

"Not nearly as bad as . . ." Angelita's voice trailed off as she looked away.

"Who? Who did you leave bleeding?" Pepper demanded.

"Well, you'll find out on Sunday at church anyway. I might as well tell you."

"Was it Matthew Harlow?"

"He's a dolt!"

"What did he do?"

"I bet him a nickel I could beat him in a race to the tracks, and —"

"You bet him? What are you doing betting with some boy? Angelita, a young lady does not go around betting!"

"Do you want to hear the part where Matthew gets a bloody nose or not?"

Pepper slumped down on the leather sofa. Angelita tagged along behind her.

"Well, tell me the whole story." Pepper patted the sofa, and Angelita bounced into place at her side.

"I beat him to the tracks fair and square, but

he wouldn't pay. He says I cheated."

"Why did he say that?"

"He said that girls aren't allowed to hold their dresses up to their knees when they run."

"You did that? You held your dress up to your knees?"

"I wanted the nickel."

"Young lady, that wasn't very discreet."

"I'm only ten and three-quarters years old. How discreet do I have to be?"

"Well, then what happened?"

"I pushed him down."

"And then?"

"Then he pushed me down. So I got up and slugged him in the stomach. He got mad and slugged me in the mouth, and my tooth came out."

"Well, we knew it was loose. I suppose it was bound to come out sooner or later. So, young lady, what did you do when your tooth came out?"

"I bloodied his nose."

"You slugged him?"

"I popped him good. It really hurt my knuckles."

"What did Master Matthew Harlow do then?"

"He ran home crying. What a baby. Look at me. I lost a tooth. My dress got dirty. But here I am, cheerful as can be — even though I didn't get my nickel."

"You wash up and come help me with supper. Mr. Andrews will be hungry this evening. I only sent a small dinner with him this morning. He said he thought it would be a long ride today."

In a few minutes, Angelita was more or less smudge-free. She teetered on a tall, unpainted wooden stool and handed down an airtight quart jar of huckleberry preserves. They both returned to the kitchen.

"I think Mr. Andrews will be home a little late for supper," Angelita announced, flipping her long braids over her shoulders as her round brown eyes danced.

With her dress sleeves rolled up to her elbows and perspiration beading her forehead, Pepper rolled out biscuit dough at the polished wood kitchen counter. "Why do you say that?"

"I saw Mr. Slaughter, and he said —"

"Where did you see Tom Slaughter?" Pepper rubbed her nose with the back of her hand.

"He was coming out of the Colorado Club, and he said —"

"What were you doing over there?" Pepper drilled.

"I, eh, it's just that . . ." Angelita put her hands on her hips and glared. "Do you want to hear what Mr. Slaughter told me or not?"

"Yes, go ahead, but you know I don't like you dawdling in front of the saloons."

"I wasn't dawdling. I mean, I don't think I even know how to dawdle. Do I?"

Pepper laughed as she cut the dough. "Go on, honey, what did Mr. Slaughter tell you?"

"He said to tell you that Tap — I mean, Mr.

23

Andrews — might be a little late for supper."

"Why is that? Is something wrong?"

"I don't think so. He said that Mr. Andrews had located some stolen cattle and that he and several men were riding out to bring the cattle back, that's all."

"Those who have stolen cattle seldom give them up easily."

"Mr. Slaughter said Tap had everything under control."

Under control? In his fashion, Lord . . . in his fashion.

"Will he be back before dark?"

"He said he'd send Mr. Andrews on home as soon as he could, because he and the other men could drive the cattle. He said that's not Tap's job."

"Was that all Mr. Slaughter said?"

"More or less."

Suddenly Angelita threw herself down on the bare wooden floor. She stretched out on her back and extended her arms and legs straight out and stared at the ceiling.

"What in the world are you doing?" Pepper demanded.

"Stretching."

"But the floor might be dirty!"

"I swept it this morning," Angelita replied. "Besides, it's cooler down here. It feels good on my back. Don't you ever like lying on the floor?"

Pepper wiped the perspiration off her forehead with an unprinted flour sack towel, debating whether to cook the biscuits now or wait until Tap arrived. "Honey, if I laid down like that, I'd never be able to get back up."

"You feeling bad?" Angelita asked.

"Oh, I get tired and winded easy. And my back always hurts."

"You want me to rub it for you?" Angelita asked.

"That would be delightful."

Angelita jumped up and scooted a chair behind Pepper. She leaped on it and rubbed Pepper's neck and back.

"Mrs. Andrews, do you like being . . . you know . . . with child?"

"Well . . . believe it or not, I do like it. But some days I get really tired and discouraged. And then I remember what it would be like for me and Tap to have a little boy —"

"Or a little girl," Angelita put in.

"Or a little girl," Pepper continued, "and then I know that it will all be worth it."

"I wonder if my mother felt miserable when I was in her tummy? She died right after I was born, you know."

Pepper turned to glance at the cheery brown face with its missing tooth. "Yes, you've told me. I would imagine whatever pain she had to go through was completely forgotten the moment she saw how beautiful you were."

Angelita's smile grew even wider. "I was probably naked when my mother first saw me."

Pepper turned to her biscuits, and Angelita

continued her back-rubbing. "Yes, that's the way we all come into this world."

"Can we go and see my daddy before school starts up?" Angelita asked.

"Tap mentioned that. Provided we save up enough money. But I don't know if I'm up to a train ride. Maybe you and he should go."

"But who would look after you?" There was a worrisome tone in her voice.

"I think I could survive a few days without you two — but only a few days."

"Well, if we do that, I don't want you to worry about Mr. Andrews. I'm sure I could keep him out of trouble," Angelita promised.

"I'm sure you could, honey, I'm sure you could."

The sun tucked itself out of sight on the distant western horizon. Light reflected off the pines on top of the southern bluffs that had given Pine Bluffs its name. The air was perfectly still and stifling. Pepper gave up fighting the assorted flying insects and left both the front and back doors of the house open, hoping for an evening drift of wind that was slow to arrive.

She and Angelita relaxed on the covered front porch that faced the dirt street. They had pulled dining table chairs out on the porch and were both working on knitting projects.

"Mrs. Andrews, I don't know why I have to learn how to knit. When I get married, my husband's going to be so rich I'll have my own private seamstress."

"But what if she goes on vacation and you need some alteration for a big ball or something?" Pepper challenged.

Angelita wrinkled her nose and looked out at the street. "Yeah . . . you might be right. But you'll need to have a better excuse next time. Did your mother teach you how to sew?"

"Not too much. My mother was sick quite a bit and died when I was fourteen. I guess I learned how to sew when I needed clothes for — for work."

"Where did you work? My mother worked at a hotel in Denver before she got married. She was a maid. Did you ever work in a hotel in Denver?"

"More or less," Pepper mumbled.

"Maybe you knew my mother. Did I ever tell you her name was Rachel? Isn't that a beautiful name?"

"Yes, I think you mentioned it. It is a beautiful name, honey. I'm sure I didn't meet your mother. I was not in Denver very long."

Your mother never came into the kind of places where I worked. It never goes away. Like faded wallpaper, you can't ever get rid of those memories, can you? Lord, give Angelita lots of very good memories that she can live with for a long, long time!

"Here he comes!" Angelita tossed her knitting aside, jumped up, and dashed out into the yard. "Hi, Mr. Andrews!"

Pepper looked up and saw Tap amble up the boardwalk toward their house. He carried his rifle

27

over his shoulder. She stepped out into the yard.

Tap grinned widely. "How are the two most beautiful women in Wyomin'?"

Pepper laughed. "I think Mr. Andrews has been looking at cows all day again. It spoils his perspective."

Angelita giggled as she clutched his right arm. "Oh, I believe he's probably right."

"What happened to you, young lady?" Tap bent over and examined Angelita's missing-tooth smile.

"I lost another one of my baby teeth. It must mean I'm getting more mature."

"Did you have a little help getting that one out?" he prodded. "What did the other kid look like when you were through?"

Angelita shrugged. "I busted his nose."

"Whose nose?" Tap glanced up at Pepper.

"Matthew Harlow. But I haven't talked to his mother yet, so I don't know his side of the story."

"He pushed me down and got my dress dirty," Angelita announced.

Tap stood up and tousled Angelita's bangs, slipping his arm around her shoulder. "Sounds like it was another exciting day in Pine Bluffs."

Pepper held on to his left arm, and the trio walked to the porch. Then she stepped back.

"You're covered with dirt, Mr. Andrews!"

"Did you get bucked off?" Angelita asked. "One time I got bucked off right into the mud. Jeremiah Gaines just stood there and laughed and laughed — until I . . ."

"Until you what?" Pepper asked.

"Eh, I better not say."

"Really, Tap, you'll need to wash up. It looks like you rolled in the dirt."

"Well, give me a few minutes, and I'll clean up and change shirts for you ladies."

"Not in my kitchen. Just wait here. I'll get the basin and bring it out. Angelita, go get Mr. Andrews's brown shirt hanging in the bedroom."

Tap leaned his Winchester against the doorjamb and hung his holstered Colt on a brass and porcelain coat hook by the open front door. Pepper returned with a basin, soap, and towel.

"I heard you found Tom Slaughter's missing cattle," Pepper commented.

"Did you see Tom?"

"Angelita did."

"Did he tell her . . ." Tap glanced at the doorway and saw Angelita, shirt in hand, violently shaking her head no.

"Did he tell her what?"

"Eh . . . that I found all sixty-four head?"

"I told you it was a perfect job for you," Pepper continued, unaware that Angelita stood in the doorway. "You get to chase cattle, talk to ranchers, and ride horseback all day. It certainly beats the tension of being a deputy in Cheyenne, to say nothing of the danger."

"Rustled cattle can be a little dangerous at times."

"Oh, well, you know what I mean. At least I don't have to sit home wondering if you're going to get shot every day."

Tap glanced over at Angelita and put his finger to his lips. Then he pulled off his shirt and stepped to the basin, his black leather suspenders hanging down the sides of his tan ducking canvas britches.

"What's that all over you?" Pepper shouted.

"Huh? Oh, these bites?"

"What happened to you?"

"Well . . . it's a long story, but basically I rolled in the dirt and ended up on top of an ant den. They bit me up one side and down the other. Have we got any rubbin' alcohol?"

"Angelita, could you run get the liniment? What do you mean, you rolled in dirt?"

"Don't tell her anything until I get back!" Angelita called out as she disappeared back into the house and quickly reappeared with a bottle in her hand. "Here." She handed it to Pepper. "Now you can go on."

Tap talked as he washed his hands, arms, neck, and face.

"Brownie went down, and I rolled across the prairie. That's about all there is to it. I ended up in some ants, and it took me awhile to brush them off. Then there was the diggin'."

Pepper took a rag, poured some rubbing alcohol on it, and began to massage it into Tap's back. "What digging?"

"Well . . . like I said, Brownie died, and I —"

Pepper's fingers dug deeper into his back. "Brownie died?"

might be a little cooler out there."

Tap settled at the end of the porch, the back of his chair leaning against the wall of the house as he sipped steaming coffee from an off-white porcelain cup.

Pepper sat next to Tap with needle and thread and a dress draped across her well-rounded stomach.

Angelita slouched in the open doorway, examining each tooth with her fingers.

"What happened to Brownie? How did he die?"

"A bullet in the head," Tap admitted.

"You had to put him down?"

"Actually someone else did the job for me."

"I'm glad someone could help you out. It's tough on you to lose him, isn't it?"

"Me and him went through a lot. Kind of like losin' a good friend."

"That's why you buried him?"

"Yep."

"Other than that, was it pretty much a routine day?" she asked.

"More or less," Tap conceded.

Angelita ran out into the yard as a young man on a sorrel horse rode up toward their house.

"Mr. Andrews!" the young man called.

"Eh . . . young Mr. Parker."

"Butch."

"Okay, Butch. Eh, this is Mrs. Andrews."

Butch tipped his round-crowned hat. "Evenin', ma'am."

"I told you he went down."

"Well, I thought you meant he stumbled."

"He died."

"You mean you rode him to death?"

"No . . . he sort of . . ."

"Sort of what?" Pepper demanded.

"What were you digging, Mr. Andrews?" Angelita interrupted. "Did you bury Brownie?"

"Yep, I did. Most folks don't bury horses in the open like that, but Brownie and me went through a lot together, so I thought it proper. Besides I had to wait for Tom Slaughter to show. He was really grateful to get all sixty-four head back."

"Did they have them rebranded?" Angelita asked.

"Yeah. You see, they took Tom's TS brand and made it into a I8I." Tap squatted down on the porch and wrote in the dust with water from the basin. "Don't ever use S in a brand, unless it's a runnin' S or a flyin' S or something like that."

He stood back up, and Pepper applied some alcohol to his chest. "If I'm not mistaken, you completely changed the subject and are avoiding telling me how Brownie died."

"Now that's a long story, and I'm nearly starved to death. I ate that dinner you put in my saddlebags about 10:30 and haven't had anything but spring water since. Let's eat, and then you can tell me about your day, and I'll tell you about mine."

"Why is it I have a feeling that your day was

much more eventful than ours?" Pepper sighed. "Put on your shirt, cowboy. Nobody eats at my table unless they're fully dressed."

Boiled potatoes, beef gravy, stewed tomatoes, fried beef chops, biscuits, and huckleberry preserves covered the small table and the plates almost as completely as the white linen tablecloth. After a leisurely supper, Tap pushed his chair back from the table and drank a third cup of coffee. Angelita gave a detailed description of her confrontation with Matthew Harlow.

"How about you, darlin'? How'd you spend your day?"

"Fat." Pepper spat the word out like a slap.

"You are not fat," Tap protested.

"You are the very man who said I was getting 'fleshed out.' "

"I meant it as a compliment."

"Mr. Andrews, let me tell you something. Calling a woman fleshed out is at no time and under absolutely no conditions ever, ever a compliment!"

"Oh."

"Mr. Andrews has a lot to learn about us women, doesn't he?" Angelita teased.

"Yes, and some days he has more to learn than other days."

"Now, look, you two, before you go hangin' me from a lamppost, make sure you know what I meant when I said that. I realize you don't like all that extra weight and your back's sore, but what I —"

"And my feet are swollen."

"Yes, and —"

"And my legs itch."

"See, what I —"

"And I can't walk two blocks without be[ing] winded."

"Yes, but —"

"And I can't sleep at night, and I've lost [my] appetite —"

"Whoa!" Tap interjected. "Let me finish [my] thought before I forget it entirely. When I [saw] that belly of yours growin', it means Little T[ap] is growing. That's good. That's really, rea[lly] good. When I said you were fleshed out, wha[t I] meant was that Little Tap —"

"Or Little Tapette," Angelita corrected.

"Yes. I meant the baby is growing fat. That[']s[a] healthy, wonderful thing."

Pepper stared at him for a minute and the[n] turned to Angelita. "What do you think, hone[y,] did he squirm out of it this time?"

Angelita nodded her head. "Yeah, nice squir[m]ing, Mr. Andrews."

"Thank you. Do you think it deserves anoth[er] cup of coffee?"

"I'll get it for you." Angelita jumped up a[nd] slipped over to the cookstove.

"Now, Mr. Andrews . . . we are still waiti[ng] for a full explanation of how Brownie died[,]" Pepper insisted.

"How about one more biscuit and jam . . . and the three of us sittin' on the front porch?[]"

"Heh . . . hum!" said Angelita.

"Oh, and this young lady is Miss Angelita Gomez, our house guest and very dear friend."

"Miss Angie." Butch nodded, and this time he pulled his hat clear off, revealing a shock of curly ash-blond hair.

"Very pleased to meet you, Mr. Parker." Angelita held her dress and curtsied.

"Butch, do we need to talk?" Tap asked.

"Yes, sir. Just for a minute."

"I'll come on out. If you ladies will excuse me and Butch, we have a little business to take care of."

"Oh, no need to be private," Butch protested. "I just wanted to bring you the reward money."

Pepper stood to her feet, clutching her mending in her hands. "What reward money?"

"Well . . . for killin' those three gunmen who tried to ambush him today, of course."

Pepper spun around and stared at Tap with her hands on her hips. "I thought you said this was just an ordinary day!"

"It was." Tap shrugged. "Except for the killin' part."

2

Onespot had always been Pepper's horse. From the day Tap had bought the little gelding from Bob McCurley, the black saddle horse preferred Pepper as his rider. With Brownie gone, Tap was left with the choice of riding the iron-gray, green-broke gelding he called Roundhouse or buy a new horse.

He and Pepper talked late into the night about the job of brand inspector, the demands of an expanding family, and how to save enough money to buy a ranch. They decided to put all three gold double eagles in the ranch account.

The next morning Tap decided against buying a new horse. Extra funds would be needed for the baby, and the rest saved for the ranch. So he cinched his saddle tight on the strong gray horse and led him around the worn split-rail corral. The horse pranced when the cinch was once more yanked tight with the full force of Andrews's 180 pounds. A burlap sack still draped Roundhouse's head. The minute Tap threw his full weight into the tapadera-covered Visalia stirrup, Roundhouse took off on a blind gallop across the corral.

Tap managed to find his seat and wildly slapped his foot in the right stirrup, at the same time yanking the gunny sack off the horse's head. Instantly Roundhouse stopped galloping and began to buck. On the third jump, the horse reversed direction in midair, and Tap lost both stirrups and his black beaver felt hat. Clutching the horn with his right hand, he hooked the horse with his spurs and hung on.

The discomfort of raking rowels did little for the horse's disposition. Roundhouse bucked even harder. Finally he bucked himself into a corner and then paused just long enough for Tap to slam his boots back into the stirrups. This time the gray took off on a trot around and around the sixty-foot square corral.

On the third pass around, Tap hollered, "Open the gate, Angelita! Let's see what he does out in the open."

She forced the gate latch up and slowly swung the sagging wooden gate wide open. Tap spurred the gray toward the opening and galloped out onto Pine Bluff's Railroad Avenue. The horse sprinted fifty yards to the west and then stopped suddenly, as if facing an uncrossable canyon. Tap was flung out of the saddle, but kept his balance by clutching the horn and the horse's black mane.

He scooted back into the saddle, turned the horse, and walked him back toward Angelita. She ran up to his side.

"Roundhouse was a lot more calm today, wasn't he?" she called out.

"Yep. I told you he'd settle down after a few days. Are you ready to ride him now?" he asked.

"Oh sure, and meet an untimely and gruesome death? I don't think it would be fair to deprive all the young men of my charm and wit, do you?"

Tap looked down at the missing-tooth smile. "You're probably right. We'll spare them all unbearable grief."

"I think I'll stick with Onespot."

Tap patted the horse on the neck. "Roundhouse will be all right as soon as I put a month of trails on him."

"A month? Every bone in your body will be broken in a month," Angelita warned.

"You're beginning to sound more like Pepper ever' day."

Angelita put hands on her hips and tilted her head sideways. "*Every* day. There's a *y* on every," she corrected.

Tap just stared. "This is startin' to get scary. Two women naggin' me. I'm surely lookin' forward to Little Tap gettin' here. That way it evens up the sides a little."

"What if it's a girl, huh? What will you do then? You'll be outnumbered three to one!"

"May the Lord have mercy on my soul."

"You've been saying that an awful lot lately."

"I need it." Tap turned Roundhouse back to the west. "Tell Mrs. Andrews that I'm ridin' northwest to Goodwin's to check out some strays they found up there. I've got enough biscuits and bacon for dinner, but I'll surely be home for supper."

Angelita shaded her brown eyes with her hand and then wiped the perspiration off her forehead with the long sleeve of her white cotton dress.

She handed Tap his dusty black hat. "It sure is hot today." She sighed.

"You're right about that, darlin'. Now don't go hangin' out in front of those stockyard saloons."

"How can I save enough money to go visit Daddy if you don't let me work in front of the saloons? Drunken drovers can be quite generous, you know."

"Yeah, and they can be mean and crazy, too. The Lord has more honorable ways for little girls to earn money."

"Mr. Andrews, I have never compromised my honor!"

Tap shook his head. "How old did you say you were?"

"I'll be eleven next month."

"Somehow I keep forgetting that." Tap grinned. "Now don't worry about the trip money to Colorado. We'll save it up some way."

"Are you going to kill any more men today?" she asked.

Tap pushed his hat back, brushed his shaggy dark hair off his forehead, and then rubbed his mustache, mouth, and chin with the palm of his hand. "I hope not, darlin'. One more gunfight and Pepper will make me quit this job and go into shopkeepin'."

"A bakery would be nice, especially one that makes cinnamon rolls."

"Keep savin' your money, and you'll be able to buy a bakery someday."

"Can I go down to the depot? It's not like the one in Cheyenne City, but it's better than nothing."

"No cheatin' or false representation, do you understand?"

Angelita stuck out her tongue, then spun around, and ran down the street.

By the time the pine-covered bluffs had dropped over the southern horizon, Roundhouse decided to give up trying to get back to the barn and settled down to a steady gait. Tap enjoyed the power of the tall, muscular horse. He had never ridden a horse that could jump out into a gallop so quickly.

The rolling prairie northwest of the tracks was covered with thick, short grass. Only a few of the lower stems still showed a hint of green. The blistering prairie sun had baked the tops brown and the roadway rock-hard.

Tap found the heat bearable, the fine, hoof-pulverized dust minimal, the wind nonexistent, and the company peaceful and contemplative.

Pepper's right. Until this land settles down more, this isn't much different from marshalin'. I never could figure who would want to die over a few head of cattle . . . and here I am puttin' my life on the line for those same bovines.

Lord, if You bring us a little Tap, Jr., I promise You he'll learn a trade. Something besides gun-slingin'.

He decided to stop to water and rest Round-house at Antelope Springs. From a distance of

40

fifty yards, he spotted two horses where the spring had kept the grass still green. Tap pulled his Winchester and laid it across the saddle horn.

One of the men tarried near his horse; the other huddled with a frying pan over a very small hot fire that was set down in a narrow trench.

"Ho, to the springs!" Tap yelled. "I'm comin' in to water my pony."

"Come on in, pard. You're welcome to join us."

The man by the buckskin gelding was short and rawboned. A two-week beard of brown hair and dirt covered his chin. His shallow eyes focused on Tap's rifle. The other man was barrel-chested and stocky. When he stood up, he had a smile as wide as his thick mustache. His eyes squinted as if he were permanently peeking out from an almost closed window.

Tap stepped down from the saddle and pulled his hobbles from around the horn. While Roundhouse drank, Tap slapped the restraints on the horse's forelegs and shoved his rifle back into the scabbard. Then he walked over to the others.

The bigger man with the thick mustache looked him right in the eyes. " 'Scuse me for starin', mister, but you remind me of someone I knew down in Arizony."

The smaller man stepped over toward him. "We jist rode up from New Mexico. Maybe you can help us find an old boy who promised us jobs. Providin' you ain't the law."

Ignoring the question, Tap continued to stare

at the bigger man. *Arizona? I don't know if I want to know this man.*

"Who you boys lookin' for?" he finally asked.

"Tap? I'll be Lucifer's uncle! You're Tap Andrews!"

Tap's right hand inched down until it rested on the walnut handle of his Colt .44.

"I heard you was killed at that massacre at Navajo Rocks."

Tap nodded his head and continued to stare. "You know, partner, I can't recollect who you are."

"Snake Dutton. I was at A.T.P. last year when you escaped."

Silvan Potter "Snake" Dutton, #392, grand larceny. A petty, whinin' horse thief, if I remember.

"Snake! No foolin'?" Tap exclaimed. "Why, you look healthy and strong. You didn't get that way in prison."

"No, sir, I wintered out with the Pueblo Indians north of Taos. Now I'm ready to go to work."

"How'd you get out of Yuma anyway?"

"The governor said it was gettin' too crowded, so he offered some of us a pardon if we'd leave the state. Seemed like a fine arrangement to me. Shoot, I should have known they didn't stop you. This here's my partner, Texas Jay."

Tap tipped his hat and noticed that the little man looked ready to draw his weapon. "Is his hand glued tight to that Colt, or is he aimin' to shoot me in the back?"

"Relax, Texas Jay," Dutton reassured. "Tap

here knows what it's like to get chased out of Arizony . . . and besides, he could kill you quicker than a hog kills a rattlesnake if you was to make a move."

"Maybe he ain't that good anymore," Texas Jay challenged.

"Well, you ain't goin' to find out today. We got work lined up, and I promised Banner two men."

As Texas Jay stalked over to the fire, Tap watched him out of the corner of his eye.

"Say, you ain't workin' for Colton Banner, are ya?"

Tap squatted down on his haunches and kept both men in view. "Afraid not. In fact, I don't even know anyone named Colton Banner. Is he runnin' cattle up this way?"

"It's north of here, from what I hear. He's got a corral up by somewhere called Lone Tree Creek."

"Lone Tree must be a hundred miles north," Tap advised.

"You don't say! I was hopin' it was a little closer. You might as well spend the nooner with us, Tap. We can talk about old Arizony."

"Thanks for the invite, Snake, but I haven't been on the trail more than an hour and a half. I better ride on."

Tap returned to Roundhouse and retrieved his almost full canteen, topping it off at the springs. Snake Dutton busied himself cooking over the fire, but Texas Jay never took his eyes off Andrews.

43

Tap walked his gray horse over by the fire. "Well, I hope you boys find this Bonner."

"Banner. Say!" Dutton shoved back his high-crowned, narrow-brimmed black hat. "You ain't lookin' for work, are ya? I heard Banner lost three men just yesterday, so I'm sure he needs more."

"Lost them? You mean his crew's quittin'?"

"Quittin' nothin'!" Texas Jay exclaimed. "They got bushwhacked."

"Oh?"

"Yep . . . a dozen or so of those Cheyenne City bummers rode into camp and leaded 'em all down."

"I heard tell they was shot right in the forehead, all three of 'em."

"Oh, where did you hear this?" Tap asked. "I didn't hear anything about an ambush."

"Some old boy who woke up broke back in Pine Bluffs came riding our way this mornin' and told us. He said a posse rode out yesterday afternoon after a hide wagon brought in the bodies. And I thought Arizony was rough."

"Are you sure those three worked for your friend Banner?"

"Well, I ain't certain, of course . . . but I heard that one of them was Dirty Al Bowlin. Dirty Al came up in the spring to work for Banner. So unless he decided to have a go on his own, he must have still been workin' for him."

"Dirty Al couldn't count his chips by himself," Texas Jay added.

"No, sir, but he surely could make that old

44

Big Fifty sing from half a mile away."

"So Dirty Al shot a Sharps .50-70?"

"Yep. I wonder what happened to that rifle? Them bushwhackers took it, no doubt."

"Where did you say Banner's headquarters is?" Tap asked. "If I get to needin' a job, I just might come up that way."

"I didn't say where his headquarters is, but we're supposed to meet his crew at the corrals at Lone Tree Crick."

"Maybe I'll look you up."

"And maybe we'll be waitin' for ya," Texas Jay responded.

"Don't mind him, Tap. He's been cantankerous ever since he got kicked out of the Pearly Gates dance hall in Denver. Say, you workin' around here?"

"I manage to keep busy." Tap nodded.

"What kind of work you doin'?"

"Oh, you know, the same old thing."

"Hirin' out your gun and chasin' them purdy ladies, are ya? That warden's wife surely was sweet on ya."

"Those days are over, Dutton. I'm a married man now." Tap reached down and tried to brush some of the trail dust off his chaps.

Rather than spit, Snake leaned his head over and let the tobacco drool from the corner of his mouth. "No foolin'? I'd never take you for the settlin'-down type."

"Well, it fits me fine now, Snake. Now if you boys will saunter back a tad — this big gray won't stand when I mount up."

Snake Dutton and Texas Jay stepped back by their little fire, and Tap swung up into the left stirrup. Long before he was able to pull his right leg over the cantle, Roundhouse bolted away from the springs and bucked his way out into the prairie. Two hundred yards later the big gray settled into a steady lope.

The afternoon turned out to be hotter, drier, and dustier than the previous one. By the time he reached the corrals surrounded by a dozen box elders at the Goodwin ranch, his leather-cased canteen was almost empty, and his gray cotton shirt was wringing wet with sweat. It took him only a minute to identify the six maverick yearlings as Two Dot T, a trail brand of Tom Slaughter's last drive up from Texas.

After a half-hour snooze under the trees, Tap cut the steers out of the corral and pushed them out onto the prairie. He figured the steers would act snuffy at Roundhouse, but they took to the trail quickly, even without a bell cow. The big gray gelding considered the affair a game to be won and refused to let any of them wander even two feet off the trail.

When they made it back to the springs, Dutton and Texas Jay had pulled out. Tap had to picket Roundhouse fifty feet from the springs in order for the steers to get a drink. The big gray seemed determined to drive them all the way to Pine Bluffs without a stop.

46

By the time they reached Tom Slaughter's corrals at the southern edge of town, Roundhouse was well lathered, and Tap was caked with sweat and dust. Leaving the steers confined in the square pen and Roundhouse turned out to the horse pasture, Tap hiked past the barn and up the boardwalk to Slaughter's office, his Winchester over his shoulder. His sweat drenched even his socks, and they rubbed his feet raw against his brown boots.

Two men in dark ties and starched-collar boiled shirts were talking to Slaughter when Tap stepped through the door.

"Sorry to bother you, Tom, but I corralled those six steers of yours that were at Goodwin's. They were Two Dot T's like you figured. I'll talk to you in the mornin'."

"Wait a minute, Tap. Step over here. I want you to meet these men." Slaughter turned to the taller of the two well-dressed men. "This is Mr. Jacob Tracker — and Mr. Wesley Cabe. Gentlemen, this is Tap Andrews, the brand inspector I was telling you about."

Tap tipped his hat at the two men.

Tom Slaughter pointed to a map laid out on his desk. The gray-headed cattle baron swooped around the office like a cougar in a cage. "Tap, Mr. Tracker and his lawyer are out of San Angelo. They're up here lookin' to buy a place for some northern summer grazin'. What they had in mind was somethin' in north Laramie County, up around Old Woman Crick. You heard about any places for sale up there?"

Tap pushed his hat back and rubbed his dirt-caked neck. "I haven't been in the Territory all that long, Tom. . . . I don't work north of the Platte very often. Afraid I can't help you. Wouldn't mind goin' up that way someday. . . . In fact, I hear there just might be some strays wanderin' up on Lone Tree Crick. Sorry, I don't know any ranchers up there, boys, but it's my firm opinion that if you have the money, every ranch in this territory is for sale. Now if I can get cleaned up enough to have the wife let me in the door, I'll go eat some supper."

Although it seemed like an impossibility to him, Tap figured it was even more oppressively hot than the previous evening. After they ate, they sat out on the porch and tried to think of cooler times.

"April's was never this hot in the summer." Pepper sighed, using her hands to fan herself. "In fact, I remember some cool summer nights when we had to close the windows and pull up the quilts."

"Well, south Arizona is hot all year 'round. I can take that. It's the cold that gets to me. Did I ever tell you about the time I spent most of one December in Bodie?" Tap asked.

Pepper glanced over at him. "What were you doing in California?"

"I was born in California, remember?"

"So was this before you went to Arizona?"

"I reckon it was about ten years ago. Ever'one was up there tryin' to cut a big slice of gold for themselves. Housin' was impossible to find, so I was cabined up with two gamblers and a, eh . . . *nymph du prairie.* Anyway —"

"A what?" Angelita asked, popping straight up in the doorway.

"Never mind, young lady," Pepper asserted.

"Oh, one of those!" Angelita rolled her big, round eyes and plopped back down.

Without glancing over at him, Pepper challenged, "Mr. Andrews, is this story going somewhere?"

"I hope so."

"So do I."

"Well, here's the thing. The wind and snow blow across the mountains at Bodie for six months at a time. It's about 20° below on a good day. It's killin' country. Forty men died in the cold one winter 'cause there wasn't any timber around for fires. Anyway, these two gamblers started up a game playin' for firewood. You couldn't buy a cord of wood for a hundred dollars, gold."

Pepper pulled her curly blonde hair up on top of her head so the back of her neck would cool off. "So you stayed warm by stoking the fire with profits from the poker game?"

"Most of the wood was probably taken from someone else's woodpile, but the evidence was burned up before anyone could complain. One time they won ten big rounds of unsplit oak. I

49

don't know who in the world hauled that valley oak clear up into the mountains, but there it was. So the gamblers decided I ought to go out into the cold and split those rounds. They didn't figure on getting calluses on their gamblin' hands, and of course we didn't want to send Posse out into the cold."

"Posse?" Pepper asked.

"Yeah, the Calico Queen — her name was 'Posse' LaFayette."

"I can see why you certainly didn't want to send her out into the cold," Pepper sniped.

"Anyway, that oak was so tight that it took me ten hours to split ten rounds. I'd swing that splittin' maul for an hour and sweat right through my clothes. Then they'd freeze solid 'til I was afraid of bustin' 'em. So I'd go thaw out my britches by the fire, then go back outside. Kept that up all day. When we finally turned the lantern out at night, Posse stuck about five of those big pieces of oak in the little potbellied stove we were using."

"She sounds quite considerate," Pepper sneered.

"You'd like her, darlin'. She reminded me a lot of Selena."

"If you remember, Selena and I didn't get along all that well."

"Oh, yeah . . . maybe I shouldn't have started this story."

"I'll leave if you want me to." Angelita's eyes opened wide.

"No, no, the story isn't, eh, delicate."

"Finish this wonderful tale, Mr. Andrews," Pepper insisted. "Miss Posse was just stoking the fire, something she undoubtedly had practice doing."

"Well, here's the thing. I'm sleepin' on the floor in my bedroll, and I wake up about midnight coughin' and hackin' 'cause the room is filled with smoke. It seems that the stove got so blasted hot that it melted the bolts on the iron door. The red-hot door fell to the floor and started smokin' the wood. I reckon a few coals popped out onto the floor, and soon the room was filled with smoke."

"What did you do then, Mr. Andrews?" Angelita asked.

"Well, I pulled on my boots and ran for the door. I shoved it open, but I couldn't get any windows open since they were all froze tight. I'd been sweatin' a lot in the heat of that room, and the minute I stepped outside, my lids froze to my eyelashes. That's when you know it's cold."

"I get shivers thinking about it," Angelita added, folding her arms over her head.

"Well, I ran back in and roused the two gamblers. One of 'em slept in a cot, the other on the table. I had to lead them out through the smoke. We stood out there coughin' our heads off. All the water was frozen, so we put out the smolderin' floor by shoveling snow back into our cabin."

"What about Miss LaFayette?" Pepper quizzed.

"Posse?" Tap grinned. "You want to know what happened to her?"

"I think I do."

"She was in the top bunk, and the air is thicker up there. She had passed out, and when I carried her outside —"

"I presume the gamblers didn't want to get their hands callused carrying a maiden in distress?"

"I didn't ask." Tap blushed. "She was a little thing. Couldn't have weighed more than a hundred pounds. I bet I could have stretched my fingers around her waist."

Pepper tried to suck in her stomach.

And just why are you talking about skinny-waisted women, Mr. Andrews?

"Anyway, she didn't seem like she was even breathin' when I toted her out. It must have looked a sight, a lady layin' out there on a blanket in the snow next to a house boilin' with smoke in 20° below zero weather and us tryin' to revive her."

"What did you have to do to revive her?" Angelita asked, her eyes fixed on Tap's.

"Never mind that," Pepper interrupted. "Did the young woman survive?"

"She pulled right out of it after we got her to breathin'. I mean to tell you, she was one grateful lady — huggin' and kissin' and . . . I mean, she really —"

"What about the cabin?" Pepper broke in. "Did it burn to the ground?"

"Nope. We shoveled snow on the hot spots, then mopped up the floor, and rebolted the stove door. It was like a steam bath the rest of the night as the snowmelt evaporated. Anyway, I gave up on Bodie a few days later and went to Arizona."

"Whatever happened to those other three?" Angelita asked. "Did you ever see them after that?"

"Never saw 'em again. I heard one of the gamblers was shot dead in El Pueblo de las Reyna de los Angeles."

"Where?"

"That's a little Spanish town between Fort Tejon and San Diego in California. And the report was the other gambler got pneumonia and died before spring right there in Bodie."

"I will probably regret asking this." Pepper faked a grin. "How about Miss Posse La-Fayette?"

"Got a letter from her one time. She said she was going to Montana to open her own place. That was years ago. But the point is —"

"You mean there is a point?" Pepper teased.

"The point is . . ." Tap noticed that he was still wearing his spurs. "If you just want a cold place to live, move to Bodie, and you'll never have to fan yourself. As for me, I'll take the summer heat over that bitter, killin' cold any day."

"Well . . . my brow is still perspiring," Pepper mused, "but it is nice to think of cold breezes. I wonder when the day will come that I've heard all your stories and adventures?"

"Probably about the time I've heard all of yours, darlin'." Tap winked at Pepper.

"That, Mr. Andrews, will never happen. There is very little of my past I ever wish to remember. And much that I will never, ever tell anyone!"

"Why's that?" Angelita asked.

Pepper gazed over at Angelita and then back out to the road. "I think those two men in the carriage are coming to our house. Are you expecting company?"

"Are you changing the subject?" Angelita questioned.

"Yes." Pepper nodded toward the carriage. "Do you know those men, Tap?"

"It looks like Tracker and Cabe. I met them over at Tom's this evenin'."

"What do they want?"

"I reckon I'll just mosey out there and ask."

Pepper watched to see if Tap was going to buckle on his holster.

He didn't.

She found herself sighing in relief.

Tracker had the bronzed face of a man who spent a lot of time outdoors.

Either chasing bovines or being chased himself.

Wrinkled, leathery skin framed the man's eyes, but not the deep hardened creases that would reveal days of staring across a hot, relentless summer desert and into blowing freezing snow. There was a toughness of smile, but not the chiseled look that comes from pushing yourself beyond exhaustion time and time again. The hands weren't overly callused. There was no missing thumb of a dally man. No rope burns at all.

'Course, nowadays anyone can call himself a cattleman.

The other man was easy to read, too. Wesley Cabe stood three or four inches shorter than Tap's six-foot frame. The eyes were cold and expressionless, fixed in a permanent inspective gaze. The face pale. The right hand soft. The mouth was set in a hard line.

Gambler and gunman . . . he's no attorney. 'Course, I've known a few gunmen who knew the law books. Carries his .45 too low to be comfortable. There's only one reason to wear your gun that low. He must plan on needing it.

"Evenin', Andrews." Tracker swung down off the carriage. Cabe stayed seated, reins in hand.

"Evenin'." Tap tipped his black hat. "What can I do for you boys?"

"Well, Andrews, I have a business proposition for you. I'd like to hire you for a couple of weeks to guide us up to the Old Woman Creek area."

"I'm much obliged to you for the confidence you have in me, but as I said down in Tom's office, I just don't know that country very well. Besides, I'm drawin' my pay from the stock association."

"I checked this out with Mr. Slaughter, and

he said they're curious about what brands are runnin' north of the Platte, so he'd take care of things down here if you wanted to go north."

"Are you tellin' me the association will keep paying my wages even though I guide you up there?"

"That's what he said. He figured guidin' us would give you an excuse for nosin' around."

"Well, that might work. And you'd pay me on top of that?"

"Fifty a week. Just think of it as a hundred-dollar bonus."

"I told you I didn't know the territory."

"Frankly, Mr. Andrews . . ." Tracker spoke softly as he glanced back at Pepper and Angelita on the porch. "The country between here and there has a reputation for being kind of wild — horse thieves, rustlers, and bank robbers on the run. What I want from you more than anything is another gun to ride with us."

"What's the matter — can't Cabe protect you?"

Wes Cabe's right hand dropped down to his revolver.

"Mr. Cabe's a lawyer."

"Look, Tracker, let's get this out in the open to begin with. Cabe has spent most of his life behind a Faro table. The barrel of that .45 has shot a few bullets, and some of them put men down." Tap waved his hands as he talked. "Now I know that. Cabe knows that. So let's don't waste time with this lawyer stuff."

A wide smile broke across Tracker's face. "Now I know for sure I want to hire you. How's sixty dollars a week sound?"

"You still haven't explained Cabe."

"Wes is a friend and business associate. And a gambler. There's no one more steady with a gun in a room full of sneakthieves and footpads . . . but out here on the prairie, it's a different matter. To be honest, we heard about your work with that '73 and long-range sight and figured it would be a good addition to our contingent."

Tap shoved his hat back and tried to stare at Tracker's eyes. The older man gazed out at the prairie behind the house. "I'll protect us if we're fired on, but I'm not a hired gun. I won't fight your fights, and I won't do your shootin' for you."

"Fair enough." Tracker scratched the back of his neck and resat his wide-brimmed gray hat. "I hope none of us have to fire a shot. Have we got a deal then?"

"I haven't heard anything out of Cabe. You don't mind Tracker's lack of confidence in your gun?"

"I didn't say that!" Tracker insisted.

"Mister, I don't care if Tracker hires an army. I'm lookin' to make some dollars here, and it don't hurt me none not to draw guard duty at night. Have you ever worked west Texas?" Cabe asked. "You sure do remind me of an old boy I used to know down there."

"I've spent the past few years mostly in Arizona."

"You don't say?" Tracker continued. "I was just down there last year and bought some Mexican beef from Stuart Brannon. Do you know Brannon?"

"Not personally," Tap admitted. "We ran, eh, in different circles. But ever'one in Arizona's heard of him. I hear he rides a big black horse that can outrun the wind."

"Yes." Tracker nodded. "Quite right. A beautiful mount."

"What's the name of that horse? I forget," Andrews baited. "It's a Spanish name, isn't it?"

"Eh . . . he calls him Diablo," Tracker replied hesitantly.

"Yeah, that's it. I always figured if I got a long-legged black stallion, I'd name him Diablo."

"Have we got a deal then? I'd like to leave in the mornin'," Tracker added.

"Well, sir, I'm a family man, so I'll need to talk it over with them first. How about me meeting you at Tom Slaughter's office about seven in the morning?"

"All right, but we'll need to leave soon after that."

"That's the best I can tell you," Tap insisted. "If you want a quicker decision, maybe you ought to keep lookin'."

"No, no. That will be fine. A man needs to talk things over with his family."

Cabe pulled off his hat and wiped his sweating pallid forehead with the sleeve of his suit coat. "Listen, Andrews, I was wonderin' — are you a Mexican?"

"Not that it matters, of course," Tracker quickly added.

"My mama was a Métis, half-French and half-Assiniboin, if you're talkin' about my *bois brulé* skin color."

"Well, your pretty daughter must take after that side of the family." Tracker took off his hat and waved it at Pepper and Angelita, who still sat on the front porch.

Tap thought about correcting the man and then decided it wasn't worth it. By the time he walked back up to the front porch, the carriage had swung around and rolled back toward the center of town.

"Well, that took awhile. What did they want?" Pepper remained seated, busy with her needlework.

"They wanted to hire me for two weeks at sixty dollars a week." Tap put his left boot on the top step and stooped to unfasten his spurs.

"That's twice what you're making now. What did they want you to do?"

"Guide them up past the Platte to look at some ranches. The one doin' the talkin' is a Texas cattleman lookin' to buy some summer grazin', I reckon." He pulled off his other spur and hung the pair on a nail by the door.

"How about the other one?"

"He's a, eh . . . business partner of sorts. Tom told 'em he'd pay me to scout around that country, too. So I could make double salary."

"We could use the money in the ranch account,

59

but would that mean you wouldn't be home for two weeks?"

"Yep. That doesn't sound too good, does it, darlin'?" Tap plopped down in the chair next to Pepper, reached over, and rubbed the back of her neck.

"It certainly doesn't."

"Here's what I'm thinkin'," Tap explained, letting his hand drop back to his side. "How about us puttin' the hundred dollars in the bank, and you two take twenty dollars for a trip to Boulder so you can visit Baltimore."

"Go see my daddy?" Angelita squealed.

"If you think you're up to it. It might be a little cooler there, and I'll be out of town anyway."

"Could we take the train?" Angelita asked.

"Yep."

Pepper dried her forehead on her sleeve. "I think we just might do that, Mr. Andrews." She smiled. "It would certainly beat sittin' here baking like a potato. A very plump potato."

"Are you sure this won't be too hard a trip for you?" he asked.

She looked down at her very round stomach. "What do you think, Lil' Tap? You want to go on a ride on the train?"

"What did he say?" Angelita asked.

"He said anywhere it's cooler is fine with him." Pepper laughed. Then she turned to Tap. "I do wish you were coming with us."

"Well, I've got to go earn the money to send you."

"When will we leave?" Angelita asked.

"I'll be headin' north first thing in the mornin'. You two might as well catch the 9:00 A.M. train to Cheyenne. You'll have to change trains there, but you know your way around that station."

"Don't remind me." Pepper stood and stretched her arms. Then she looked at Angelita. "Well, come on, honey, we've got to go pack."

"I can't believe this!" Angelita giggled. "It's like an answer to my prayers . . . you know, if I prayed as much as you two."

"So you aren't the praying type?" Tap asked her.

"I'm very self-sufficient, so I don't need to bother the Lord very often," she explained.

"How about when your daddy was shot? Did you pray then?"

"Okay, so most of the time I'm self-sufficient."

"And what about when Del Gatto used you for a shield?"

"Well, I did pray that he wouldn't shoot me when I dropped to the ground."

"Well, maybe this trip is an answer to your prayers, young lady," he suggested.

"I suppose." She wrinkled her nose. "There's a possibility you could be right."

"Thank you."

"You're welcome."

The evening was warm, stuffy, and hectic, but the time passed quickly as Pepper and Angelita prepared for their trip to Colorado. Tap was still

61

awake when Pepper finally crawled into bed. He could tell from her sigh that she was exhausted, so he didn't bother talking. When the lantern flickered out, he lay on his back and reviewed the same thoughts that had occupied his mind for the past hour.

Ever'one in Arizona knows that Brannon's horse is El Viento. Stuart Brannon is one man who would never, ever call his horse El Diablo — the devil. Tracker doesn't know Brannon at all. That was just a big windy. Why did he need to lie to me? But as long as I get my pay and don't have to do anythin' illegal . . .

Maybe I should tell Pepper about my suspicions, but she'd fret over it.

Lord, that lady worries too much.

I hope.

3

Mornings.

//The only faintly cool part of a late August day in eastern Wyoming Territory was the first two hours of daylight. From before the sun came up until about an hour afterwards, even a windless day had a cool drift about it.

Tap had Roundhouse bucked out before Tracker and Cabe showed up at the corrals. He cleared things with Tom Slaughter and took a twenty-dollar advance back to Pepper and Angelita for their traveling expenses.

Alone with Pepper on the front porch, he had given her a last long, soft kiss. Then he mounted a prancing Roundhouse and galloped back to the corrals.

My, how that woman can kiss.

I do believe they're even sweeter when she's in the family way. 'Course, I never kissed a gal in that condition before.

At least, not that I know of.

Tracker and Cabe had a buckboard packed by the time he returned, and they rolled out of Pine Bluffs just as the last vestige of morning coolness vanished. The road north varied in width and condition. It was neither a stage nor a military route. Of the 20,789 people who inhabited the entire Territory of Wyoming, extremely few lived along its eastern boundary. During the first hour on the trail, Tap counted three ranch headquarters. After that there were none.

He rode the big gray about two lengths ahead of the buckboard. The dust from the wagon wheels boiled up about fifteen feet into the air and seemed to hang forever. The prairie was devoid of trees, and the rolling brown grass was broken up only by an occasional clump of granite rock or a defiant prickly pear cactus.

Spring Creek still had a few potholes with standing water, and Tap made sure the horses got watered. It was past noon when they reached the chaparral near the head of Bushnell Creek. Scattered scrub cedar, piñon pines, and yucca littered the rocky hillside, bringing the first variance of vegetation since they left Pine Bluffs.

"Andrews, you do plan on stoppin' to eat, don't you?" Jacob Tracker called out.

Tap circled the big gray back to the wagon. "That clump of cedars over there is just about as much shade as you're goin' to find till we hit Horse Creek. You might as well noon it there. I've got a stash of hardtack and jerky, so I think I'll ride up there to that butte and take a look around."

"You aren't going to stop and stretch?" Cabe quizzed with an almost demanding tone.

Kind of pushy, aren't you, Cabe? I trust you about as much as a wasp in my britches.

"I've been in the saddle most ever' day for the past three months. After a while it kind of gets to feelin' like sittin' in a rockin' chair on the front

64

porch. Anyway, this country is mighty pretty, and someday it will make an ace of a ranch. But right now it's about the only place in a hundred miles where you could hide some stolen cattle. So as brand inspector, I better check around a little. I'm sure you two can fork down some fixin's and take a nap without me around."

"I'd be interested in knowing if you run across any tanks or springs in here," Tracker informed him. "If I drive cattle through here, I need to know where water is."

"I can tell you one thing. You better drive 'em before August. It can get mighty dry out here."

"When are you goin' to be back?" Cabe demanded.

Tap glared at him for a minute. "Just relax, Cabe. Why don't you go mark some cards or oil your hair or file your fingernails — whatever it is you do."

Wes Cabe bristled at the words, his deep, baggy eyes failing to disguise the hatred.

"And if I were you, I'd stay out of the sun. Your neck's gettin' mighty red already," Tap added.

Andrews turned Roundhouse away from the buckboard and trotted up the side of the hill. He could feel the power in the horse's hips as the big gray scampered up the incline with an eagerness that belied four hours on the trail.

The highest point in the hill country proved to be a rocky butte that jutted up about thirty feet higher than the ground around it. A lone cedar grew at its base, and Tap tied Roundhouse up to the tree and pulled off his saddle.

"Stay in the shade, big boy, and you'll feel a lot better this afternoon. I'll water you up good when we get to Horse Crick."

Tap took his rifle with him and hiked to the top of the rocks. He sat down facing west and pulled off his hat and set it on a rock, crown down. He untied his red bandanna, searched for a clean and fairly dry spot on it, and wiped his forehead and neck before he retied it. Then he jammed his hat back on. With the rifle lying across his lap, he surveyed the countryside.

Lots of protection from the wind and snow in the winter time. A man could run a thousand head back in these little canyons and draws. 'Course, he'd need to winter feed. Maybe grow some hay out on the prairie and build a barn right down on Bushnell Crick. None of 'em like to winter feed, but then the winters have been mild. Not that I want a ranch in this country, Lord. . . . Well, actually I'll take a ranch in about any old country you give me — as long as I can feed Pepper and Angelita and the baby and me.

He stood up and turned slowly north, trying to fix his mind on every landmark, arroyo, and clump of trees.

A couple dozen here . . . a couple dozen there . . . a gang could cache a fairly sizable herd in here, provided they were willing to round them all up later on. Only problem is, what would they do with them? Drive 'em to the Black Hills, I suppose. Sell them to the prospectors and miners. But they'd have to cross the North Platte. If a man has to do all that work, he might as well get a legal job. Never could figure out rustlin'. The pay's lousy, work's tough, hours long, and the chances of growin' old mighty slim. Kind of like hittin' yourself in the head with a hammer.

When he turned east, he was surprised to see a low cloud of dust out near the Nebraska line. He studied the horizon for several minutes.

"Either someone's pushin' a head of cattle or . . ."

Tap rubbed the sweat off his mustache, pushed his hat back, and watched the dust cloud as it crept westward.

They stopped? Cattle don't stop all at once like that. It's got to be . . .

Suddenly a tiny cloud of dust branched off to the southwest. Tap traced the line forward into the chaparral.

Tracker and Cabe's fire! They're sending scouts to check out that fire. Sioux? Cheyenne? Arapaho? Crow? Maybe Sioux that dropped down out of Dakota.

Tap trotted down the butte toting his rifle over his shoulder.

"I should have left you saddled. Listen, you hardheaded, oversized pony, stand still and let me get to work!"

He had to neck Roundhouse to the tree in order to get the gelding to quit shying away from the saddle. When Tap jerked the cinch tight,

Roundhouse kicked at him and caught Andrews right above the knee on his left leg.

Tap clutched his leg and staggered around the hillside.

Tears of pain plowed through the dirt on his cheeks.

"You pinheaded, over-muscled . . . sorry excuse for a horse!" Andrews shouted. "I should never have given up cussin'! You just about broke my leg!"

Andrews reeled back to the tethered horse and loosened the lead rope from the tree. Clutching the latigo for support, he painfully led the irresolute horse down into a clearing and then stared for a minute at the saddle horn that suddenly seemed higher than he remembered.

"Why did you kick my left knee? I can't put any weight on it, so how on earth am I going to mount you on the run? 'Course, I could climb up on the right." Tap winced as a sharp pain shot through his left knee and into his leg.

He stepped in front of Roundhouse and reached around the horse's neck to bring the reins to the right side.

"Okay, if I take much longer, Tracker and Cabe will do something dumb and end up gettin' that canyon named in their memory. I'm mounting from the off side, and you're goin' to stand . . . do you understand that?"

Roundhouse's ears stood straight, and he peered back showing some white in his eyes.

"Why is it I think I'm goin' to regret this?"

Tap found it extremely painful to lift his right leg and shift all his weight to his injured left. With his right hand gripping both the reins and the saddle horn, Tap shoved his right boot into the tapadera-covered stirrup and took a deep breath.

"All right, knucklehead, let's see what happens now."

To his utter surprise, Roundhouse stood perfectly still as he mounted. Even when Tap gingerly shoved his left foot into the stirrup, the horse didn't move a hoof.

"Well, I'll be! You're an Indian pony, Roundhouse! This isn't the first time you've been mounted from that side, is it? Come on, cayuse, let's go earn our pay . . . if it's not too late."

Tap could feel the rhythm of his heartbeat in the painful throbs of his left knee, but he had little time to think about it as he spurred the horse down the coulee, through the trees, and up the other side. With his Winchester in his lap, he circled the column of smoke and came up on Tracker and Cabe from the south side.

Two young Indian men in buckskin britches and white cotton shirts with purple sashes for belts stood defiantly back to back as Tracker and Cabe circled them with guns drawn. The braves had their thick black hair cut at the shoulders, with bangs hanging almost to their defiant dark eyes.

"It's about time you showed up," Cabe growled. "These two tried to raid our camp."

Tap rode straight up to the four men but remained mounted. "They try to steal something?"

"No." Tracker kept his eyes focused on the two Indians. "But Cabe stopped them before they got a chance to try anything."

"I thought you were gettin' paid for doin' this," Cabe complained.

"What I'm gettin' paid for is to save your lives, and that's what I'm about to do."

"What do you mean, save our lives? They're the ones about to die," Cabe boasted.

"What do you suggest?" Tracker glanced up at Tap for a split second.

"I want you two to holster your guns, apologize for your rudeness, give them something to eat, and tell them they can have this campsite because we're leavin'."

"Like the devil, I will," Cabe protested. "They ain't gettin' nothin' from me but a hunk of lead." He raised his revolver straight up at one Indian's head. The young man promptly spat in Cabe's face. But before Cabe could respond, the barrel of Andrews's '73 rifle slammed up against the gambler's head.

"Drop it, Cabe!" Andrews shouted.

"I ain't about to."

"I said drop it right now, or so help me, I'll blow your head off!"

"I should have known a breed like you would stick up for Injuns!" Cabe lowered his arm to his side, but he kept the gun in hand.

"What do you think you're doin'?" Tracker asked.

Both Indians stared up at Tap.

"I'll tell you in five minutes. Right now follow my lead. Cabe, I'm talkin' to you. Don't do something dumb. These boys understand every word we speak. Don't you, boys?"

The Indians glanced at each other but didn't say anything.

"Well," Tap continued, "my friends and I are extremely sorry for the rude reception. Some less honorable men have been stealing cattle in this area, and you were mistaken for them."

"What?" Cabe groused.

Tap swept his arm toward the fire. "We would like to give you a present of this food and this fire. We are leavin' this land and goin' north. May you and your people have a pleasant stay in these hills."

"Their people? There's more of them?" Tracker gasped.

"Leave the food but pack up the dishes. Cabe, go hitch the team quickly."

"I ain't goin' to start takin' orders from you," he sneered.

"Well, I am," Tracker admitted. "This is exactly the reason I wanted Andrews along."

"Do you boys understand what I said?" Tap addressed the Indians.

"Yes, we understand," the taller of the two responded. Then the other spoke something in Sioux. "He said, 'The one at the wagon will never

71

live to be an old man.' "

"That's probably true, boys, but he won't die today," Tap asserted.

"No. He will not die today. We will go tell the people."

"Take the food with you as a gift," Tap insisted. "Give them that pot, Tracker."

"Eh, but it's the only large one we have."

"If you're dead, you won't need a pot at all."

"You're right about that."

"Toss the biscuits on the top and hand them the sack of dried apples."

The two Indians accepted the food, then mounted their ponies, and galloped off to the east just as Cabe circled up to the fire with the wagon.

"You owe us a lot of explaining, Andrews! I could've shot them two Indians dead, and you know it. Ain't nobody goin' to back me off and then walk away clean. You'll pay, Andrews! It's goin' to cost ya!"

"How many are out there?" Tracker asked.

"At least three hundred."

"Three hundred!"

"That's men, women, and kids. Looks like they're headed for these trees for a summer camp."

"But this is miles and miles from the reservation! They can't come here," Cabe protested. "They have to stay on that reservation or be shot."

"We aren't the ones to shoot them. We'll let

the Indian agents and the boys in blue handle Indian matters."

"What took you so long gettin' back? We could've had all three hundred of 'em on us before you returned," Cabe complained. "Maybe you was hopin' they'd ambush us."

Tap ignored Cabe and looked right at Jacob Tracker as he talked. "Yeah . . . well . . . my horse kicked my left leg so hard it liked to cripple me. I won't wander off so far next time."

"Why didn't you tell us all that when you first rode up?" Tracker questioned.

"Because it's better to treat Indians right because you want to rather than because you're scared to death of 'em. This way we were generous. They owe us something, and they won't forget. If they think you gave it up just to save your hide . . . well, it's their tribute, and they don't owe you anything."

"If you'd let me shoot those two, we wouldn't have lost anything. We can surely outrun a whole village of savages."

"For how long?" Tap asked. "If you two are serious about a ranch up here, you'd better start makin' all the friends you can — no matter what color they are."

"Andrews is right, Wes. There's no way we need trouble on the first day out."

"Or any day," Tap added.

"Right. We aren't lookin' for any trouble, that's for sure."

Tap stared at Tracker's narrow eyes. *And just*

They made camp between three cottonwoods that marked the big bend in Horse Creek. Tap volunteered to tend the fire if the other two took the cooking chores, limited now to what could be done with a coffeepot and frying pan.

Tap had gingerly slid down out of the saddle, trying to keep all his weight on his right leg. He succeeded in pulling the tack off Roundhouse and getting the horse picketed for the night. While scrounging up some firewood, he heard a noise behind him and whirled around on his left foot.

The excruciating pain shooting up his leg caused him to collapse on the ground and clutch his knee. He lay on his back and looked up at the clear Wyoming sky. He could feel a tear slip out of the corner of his left eye.

Lord, I surely didn't need this. Not kicked by a horse! I've been stabbed, shot, and snake-bit, but it didn't hurt this bad.

Andrews struggled to his feet.

If You've got a purpose for this, Lord, I reckon it would ease the pain just a little to know what it is. Yes, sir, I think that might help a tad.

They decided to set a night watch just in case a few Sioux wandered north to check out their location. Tap volunteered for the first shift and had no objections from the other two.

It had been dark for a couple of hours before Tracker and Cabe decided to turn in. Wes Cabe chose the back of the buckboard. Tracker tossed out his roll underneath. Tap spread his bedroll across the clearing about twenty-five feet away from the other two.

"You ain't bein' too sociable," Cabe complained.

"Well, boys, it's to your advantage."

"How's that?" Tracker asked.

"We don't have enough wood, and anyway it's too blame hot to keep a fire goin'. And from time to time I have nightmares . . . you know, dreamin' about old gunfights and such. Well, since I always sleep with my Colt in my hand, I have a tendency to sit up and start shootin' at anything that moves. It's a nasty habit."

"Good grief, I should say so!" Tracker exclaimed.

"Don't worry. I can go six months without that ever happening at all."

"How long's it been since you had one of those attacks?" Cabe asked.

"I haven't been bothered with it since right after the first of the year. That's why I like the first shift at night guard. Then you don't have to come wake me up in the night. I just want to tell you right now, it ain't nothin' personal."

"You can just sleep over there as far as you want," Jacob Tracker insisted.

"Thank ya. . . . I'll wake you up, Cabe — about midnight."

"You got a pocket watch?"

"Nope. Don't need one."

"How will you know when it's midnight?"

"Trust me. Now I'm goin' to kick out the fire. I'll be leanin' against that big cottonwood stump. If you plan on wanderin' around over that way, be sure and 'hello' to me first."

Tap sprawled on his bedroll, his back against the stump and the rifle across his lap. He found that if he propped his left leg up on his saddle, once the initial jolt of pain shot through his body, the leg actually felt better. Although it was a moonless night, the blanket of stars provided enough light to see the outline of the wagon straight ahead of him and silhouettes of the three horses as they grazed and slept standing.

This is goin' to be a long two weeks if Cabe keeps totin' that chip. 'Course, I don't mind comin' out with another $120. But I'm goin' to need a lot more. Government land bein' $1.25 an acre, a 5,000 acre place would be, eh . . . over $6,000 . . . $6,250. The bank wants 30 percent down, which would make . . . I can't even write in the dirt and read it at night. Let's see, one . . . eight . . . seventy-five . . . $1,875. If I can get anyone to take a chance on me. 'Course, I'd need some start-up money at $21 a head. Maybe a hundred cows and a couple bulls . . . maybe $2,000, if I'm lucky — barn, corrals, windmill, well — oh, yeah, and a house.

Any way you cut it, Andrews, you need $5,000 to have a decent place. So far, countin' the double eagles and the $120, we have saved about $320 in six months of being married. At this rate, providin' expenses don't go up too much, it will take almost eight years!

That can't be right.
Is that right?
The baby will be half-grown.
I must've made a mistake.

Most of the next three hours he spent refining and refiguring the numbers over and over. Tap didn't get any closer to owning a ranch, but it did keep him awake through an otherwise uneventful shift.

Cabe decided to keep guard by sitting up in the wagon. Tap knew where that would lead but didn't protest. Back by his stump, he lay on his bedroll, his Colt in his right hand, his Winchester by his left side, his hat hanging on his saddle horn, his boots still on his feet, and his left knee throbbing.

Tap's left leg had so stiffened by morning that he had to drag it around as he started up a campfire. The warmth from the flames limbered it a little after he rubbed on some liniment that Pepper had insisted he bring to treat the lingering effects of his ant bites. The coffee was boiling by the time Tracker crawled out from under the wagon.

The slightly bowlegged and graying Jacob Tracker stretched his arms, combed his hair with his fingers, and jammed his worn black hat tight on his head as he approached the fire.

"Wes never roused me. You didn't take my shift, did ya?"

"Nope. Cabe decided to take his shift asleep,

but ever'thing turned out fine. It takes discipline for a tired man to sit up at night and stare into the dark."

"Discipline or fear. Back in the old days in Texas, I sat up with my daddy three nights in a row staring at the night and listening to taunts from the Comanches. You can keep your eyelids open a lot longer if you plan on gettin' scalped the moment you shut 'em. You figure we'll make it to the North Platte tonight?"

"Yep. It shouldn't be too hard to cross in late August."

"How close will that put us to Ft. Laramie?"

"I'd judge it at about twenty miles. You two got business at the Fort?"

"Nope. After we cross the North Platte, how far will it be?" Tracker quizzed.

"From what I hear, one day north ought to take us to Hat Crick Breaks, and then we'll start down the Old Woman Crick drainage about the time we draw up even with the Dakota line."

"I don't want us to wander over into Nebraska. I'm strictly interested in Wyomin' land."

"You'll know when you're in Nebraska. Nothin' in that part of the state but the Sand Hills. About noon I'll need to pull off and ride up Lone Tree Creek just in case some cattle grazed this far north."

"We'll be a long ways from Pine Bluffs."

"Well, them bovines have a tendency to really wander off when someone rebrands them and pushes them up the trail."

78

"You goin' to need some help?"

"Nah, I'm lookin' for cattle, not a fight. This far from home, I don't aim to start anything. I'll just scout it out and give the stock association a report. They can figure out what they want to do."

Wes Cabe finally dragged himself out of the buckboard, mumbled a few words to Tracker, and ignored Andrews completely. He spent most of the next half hour staring at a blue tin coffee cup he held in his hands. The sun was already visible on the eastern prairie when they finally got the wagon loaded. Tap mounted Roundhouse on the off side and once again found the horse perfectly calm while he painfully climbed into the saddle.

But the minute his backside hit the leather, the big gray started to buck. Two wild jumps toward the buckboard, and the team of horses broke into an instant gallop, leaving Tracker straining for control and Cabe tumbling to the back of the wagon.

If he hadn't been fighting to keep from getting dumped himself, Tap could have enjoyed a good laugh. As it was, he was glad that after half a dozen jumps, Roundhouse slipped into a lope and allowed him a slight degree of control.

The sun blazed straight overhead when they stopped at the mouth of Lone Tree Creek. Tap gave Roundhouse a rest and refilled his canteen before he mounted, left the others, and rode southwest up the almost dry creekbed. Even though it was as hot as on previous days, a slight breeze blew right into Tap's face. The wind seemed to invigorate the gray horse. He high-stepped and pranced most of the way.

"You feelin' that good, boy? I'd like to race you one of these days at the Fourth of July picnic. There's no way they could beat you at a distance . . . but then I don't know if I could hold on for the distance."

Lone Tree Creek seemed to Tap to be a misnomer. He couldn't find a tree anywhere. Where the creek emptied into Horse Creek, it was just a wide swell in the rolling prairie. In August it was no more than three feet wide and about six inches deep. As he rode upstream, Tap figured that somewhere out on the prairie there must be a spring or two that kept the water running.

Most of the countryside was rolling prairie with draws and swells not more than twelve feet deep. Each one could have held several hidden riders, but none was large enough for a corral or a hideout.

Dutton and Texas Jay said they were to meet someone at the corrals on Lone Tree Creek. But this might be the wrong creek. Horse Creek . . . Bear Creek . . . Lone Tree Creek. This should be it.

Tap watched the mud along the creek and stopped sporadically to investigate the cattle and horse tracks.

Spring roundup's finished; fall roundup's still months away . . . there's too much activity out here, and they don't look like Indian ponies.

The rolling prairie began a precipitous rise away from the creek, and Tap soon found himself riding into what was almost a canyon. The walls were still rolling brown-grass-covered prairie, but it would be hidden unless a person rode straight into it.

"Roundy, ol' boy, if this draw gets a little more vertical, it would make a natural corral. Just post a couple men downstream here, and you could hold a pen full of cows for weeks without anyone knowin' it."

On the southern horizon, Tap spotted two riders cresting the prairie. They rode down into the coulee about half a mile ahead of him. He cocked his lever-action rifle and laid it back down on his lap and shut Roundhouse down to a slow walk. The riders kept their horses ten to fifteen feet apart. They turned toward Tap and waited for his arrival.

The clean-shaven one on the left wore a dark wide-brimmed felt hat with a Montana crease, a long-sleeved white cotton pullover shirt, and a black leather vest. He sat straight up in his California saddle. The reins draped through the fingers of his left hand, which rested on the slim silver saddle horn. His right hand leaned against the horse's rump only a few inches from a holstered Colt .44.

The cowboy on the right had a mustache that seemed to droop clear to the bottom of his chin. He was older and heavier. He wore a floppy gray hat that looked permanently raised up in the front. His brown and white paint horse was small for the north country. A turquoise and silver hackamore encircled the horse's nose. In the rider's lap lay a '66 Winchester rifle, its copper and tin gunmetal receiver reflecting the bright sun. Tap couldn't see if this man carried a revolver or not.

As he got closer, Tap watched the younger man glance over at the older one.

Okay, Mr. Bent Hat, you're callin' this one. Make your move.

Tap was about fifty feet away when the older one shouted, "That's far enough, pilgrim. This is private property. I'm afraid you'll have to turn around."

Tap stopped Roundhouse and kept his eye fixed on the older man. "I was lookin' for a corral."

"Ain't no corral here, so just turn around and keep on riding."

"No corral? I was told there was a corral on Lone Tree Crick."

"You was told wrong."

"That could be. But Snake Dutton and Texas Jay said a cowhand might find some work up here. Said to meet the boss at the corrals. I don't know my way around in this country, boys. You haven't seen Snake and Texas Jay, have you? Just point me in the right direction, and I'll surely hightail it out of here."

The men glanced at each other. Then the older

one pushed his hat back with his left hand but never took his right off the trigger of the carbine.

"What did you say your name was?"

"Andrews."

"Ain't I seen you somewhere before?"

"You been in Arizona?" Tap asked.

"Nope."

"Me and Snake were down there in prison in Yuma a year or so ago."

"You been in Colorado?"

Tap watched the man's dark brown eyes. "Yep."

"Rico Springs! That's it!" The man spit tobacco off to the right, never taking his eyes off Tap.

If that carbine moves three inches to the left, I'm pullin' this trigger, mister.

"I remember you. I won two dollars off you when Big Karl tangled with that Texas gunslinger last fall. Remember, they fought it out in the street. Both of 'em nearly died."

"The whole thing's a vague memory." Tap nodded. "But you're right, I was there."

"Shoot, why didn't you say you were one of the Rico Springs boys?"

"I only stayed there that one night."

"No foolin'? I holed up there for two winters. But no more. Did you know that April's Dance Hall burned to the ground?"

"That's what I heard."

"Colorado's gettin' too civil, if you know what I mean. Wyoming, Montana, Idaho . . . Arizona

— them's about the only places left for a man to stretch."

"We lettin' him ride in or not?" the younger man asked his trail partner. "Banner said he wanted nine men here, and we got eight. But he's the only one who does the hirin'. We're just loafin' around until Monday when he comes in. You can stay with us if you want, but we ain't promisin' you no job."

"And if Colton don't like ya, he'll probably shoot ya," the other man added.

"Don't sound like too good an outfit to work for," Tap commented.

"We work for two dollars a day plus a percentage of the cattle sales. That ain't bad."

These guys are probably pullin' in more than a brand inspector makes. No wonder this Banner gets 'em to sign up.

"I guess I'll just have to ride on then. Give my regards to Snake and Texas Jay."

"They ain't here right at the moment. They lost their poke in a monte game last night and went to the bank for a withdrawal."

"There's no town for a hundred miles except Ft. Laramie."

"That might be, but I speculate they'll come home with some jingle."

"Adios, boys."

"See you, Andrews."

As Tap turned to ride away from the two gunmen, he heard the younger one say, "Hey . . . wasn't that deputy in Cheyenne City called

84

Andrews? You know, the one that killed that big bartender that worked for Del Gatto?"

Tap kept riding but slipped his hand down onto the handle of his revolver.

"That was Anderson. What was his first name? It was a Mexican name . . . Reata . . . Reata Anderson."

Reata Anderson? Lord, I do believe You confused their minds. 'Course, with these two it probably didn't challenge You much.

If Dutton and Texas Jay are on the prowl for someone to rob, they just might come across Tracker and Cabe. This is gettin' mighty complex.

Tap had instructed Jacob Tracker to follow Horse Creek all the way to the North Platte. It was shorter to keep going straight when the creek turned east, but Andrews figured it would be an easier journey along the creek and would give him time to catch up with them.

When he came to the bend in the creek, he spotted fresh wagon tracks climbing the embankment and heading north.

"I'll bet you two bits, Roundhouse, that it was Cabe's idea to go north. He surely resents me coming along. But they're out in the open, and it can't be more than ten miles to the river. They won't get lost."

About two miles from Horse Creek, Tap noticed hoofprints indicating that two riders from the west had begun to follow the buckboard.

Sometimes I hate being right. Play it smart, boys. Wait until dark — or at least until I ride up.

Tap followed both sets of prints for another mile. Then he noticed that the horses had swung off to the left, entering a fairly deep but narrow coulee.

Swinging around for an ambush, no doubt. Boys, you are as predictable as a pretty girl in springtime.

Tap nudged Roundhouse from a lope to a trot as he traced the wagon wheel prints in the dry prairie soil. Although he could see the trees alongside the North Platte a few miles ahead on the distant horizon, the buckboard had dropped out of sight among the swells and draws in the rolling prairie.

Two gunshots rang out in the stillness of the afternoon. Tap spurred Roundhouse to a gallop. Boiling over the crest of a knoll, Andrews came upon Cabe and Tracker hiding behind their buckboard and firing at two large boulders about one hundred feet away. The two granite rocks were the only ones for miles and looked as if they had been dropped straight out of heaven.

Tap rode to the top of the knoll above and behind the wagon where he could overlook the entire scene. He aimed his rifle at the boulders and fired a shot close to a jagged edge of the granite to shower the pair with rock chips.

Cabe and Tracker spun around toward him, but he didn't take his eyes off the boulders.

"Snake!" he hollered. "Is that you and Texas Jay back there?"

"Who's out there?" a voice yelled back.

"It's me — Tap Andrews. Those are my friends

down there, and I'll have to shoot ya if you keep this up."

"I thought you and me was friends!"

"I won't let them shoot you either."

"We didn't know they was your friends."

"You know now!" Tap hollered, never taking his finger off the trigger nor his eye off the rocks. "You two just mount up and ride on down the trail. No reason for anyone to carry lead today."

"What if we don't want to go?" It was a higher-pitched voice that Tap figured belonged to Texas Jay.

"Then you'll force me to shoot you both."

"You ain't that good."

"Of course I am. Just ask Snake. Now I'm sorry that you lost your pokes in a monte game, but I can't allow you to rob my friends."

"How'd you know that?" Dutton called.

"I went visitin' with the boys at the corral on Lone Tree Crick."

"You sign up with Banner?"

"Not yet, but the pay sounds good. I'm workin' for Tracker down here at the buckboard right now. Make up your mind, boys. Day's gettin' late. You want to ride off, or want me to write to your mamas?"

There was a long pause. No guns were fired.

"We're goin' to leave, Andrews."

"Good choice, Snake."

"Don't let them take a shot at us."

"They won't."

"I ain't through with you, Andrews!" Texas Jay shouted from behind the rock.

"Get him out of here, Snake."

"We're goin'!"

The two gunmen scampered from behind the rocks to their waiting horses. Tap eased Roundhouse down off the knoll toward Tracker and Cabe. His stirrups were swung up by the horse's neck to keep him from sliding forward as they descended. He still carried the rifle across his lap. His left leg throbbed as his weight shifted from the seat of the saddle to the stirrups.

Both men still had their revolvers pointing toward the boulders.

" 'Bout time you showed up," Cabe complained. "How come you always wander off right before trouble starts? A man might think you had it planned that way."

"Why is it you two didn't follow Horse Crick like I instructed?" Tap questioned.

" 'Cause this way is miles shorter," Cabe informed him.

Tap scanned the horizon while he talked. "Looks to me like you wasted time goin' this way. You don't make many miles standin' around shootin' at rocks."

"Andrews is right about that," Tracker responded, holstering his gun and stepping up to inspect the rigging on the team of horses.

"We were holdin' our own," Cabe insisted.

"That's because Dutton and Texas Jay are buffoons."

"Are you sayin' we can't face down real gun-men like you?"

"What I'm sayin' is that if they had half a brain between them, they would have laid up there on that knoll and picked you off before you knew they were there."

"Can't argue that, Wes. Come on, let's get on up to the North Platte. I've had enough excitement for one day," Tracker pressed.

Both men loaded back into the buckboard.

"You boys lead the way. I'll drop back here to make sure those two aren't followin' behind," Tap called out.

"I'd rather you were up ahead where I can keep an eye on you!" Cabe hollered.

"Guess you'll just have to turn around." Tap tipped his hat.

Two days is about it, Cabe. How in the world will I last two weeks with you?

Wes Cabe kept sporadically looking back as the wagon rolled along. Tap's attention focused on the shifting shadows cast by the western slope of the prairie. Rather than look back, he glanced to his left side. He cocked the hammer back on the rifle and pulled the long-range sight down out of the way.

"Take it easy, boy," he said softly to the big gray horse. "It's goin' to sound loud, but it won't hurt you."

A hat and head silhouette bobbed above the shadow of the knoll.

Texas Jay, I can't believe you have lived this long.

No one sets an ambush with the sun behind his back.

Then the hat, head, and shoulders shadow appeared. Someone was standing in the stirrups up on the knoll, pointing a carbine down the slope.

"Andrews!" the rider shouted.

4

Tap whirled in the saddle with his rifle to his shoulder. The metal gun sights fanned the horizon and locked on the silhouetted rider.

Don't do it, Texas Jay. Nobody's that dumb.

An explosion sounded from a carbine on the knoll.

Andrews's '73 Winchester blasted in return.

A bullet cuffed the dirt ahead of the big gray horse.

Roundhouse hurtled toward the wagon.

The gunman on the knoll plunged backwards off his saddle into the baked, dry Wyoming prairie . . . and eternity.

Tap clenched the reins and snapped the panicked horse's head to the left and began to circle him. Tracker and Cabe piled out of the wagon with guns drawn and took cover.

Lord, it's like I get throwed from one crisis to another.

"Settle down, boy . . . settle down. Whoa, boy . . . it's okay." He stopped the horse from spinning and patted the gray's fear-tightened neck.

There's got to be a peaceful life and a peaceful horse — somewhere.

With Roundhouse back in control, Tap hollered, "It's all right, boys. Nothing to worry about now. Let's get on up to the river."

"What about the other one?" Cabe bellowed

from a safe position behind the buckboard.

"He won't follow. Not even Snake Dutton is that dumb."

They reached the North Platte within the hour. Tap turned them east toward the Nebraska line. Not much deeper than a foot, the river ran a sandy, caramel color and stretched a good hundred feet across. Willow, box elder, cottonwood, and ash trees lined both banks, with brush thick between them.

One man couldn't work that brush. Not at this time of the year with all the trees and bushes leafed out. There's enough cover to hide cattle or rustlers or both. Someone ought to come up here in the winter and burn the brush.

But not me.

The river provided a ribbon of greenery in an otherwise buckskin-colored landscape under an expansive blue Wyoming sky. Tap could feel his bandanna droop with sweat as he bounced and swayed in rhythm to Roundhouse's steady trot. With toes hooked in the stirrups, knees pressed lightly against the horse's flanks, back as straight as a schoolteacher's ruler, he surveyed the distant horizon.

Downriver a building came into view. Tracker stopped the wagon and waited for Tap to catch up.

"What's up ahead?"

"Ought to be Shaver's Crossing. A little store and a ferry, I think. A friend of mine freights up here sometimes. He didn't recommend the place.

We could cross the river anywhere at this time of year. But you might want to put the wagon on the ferry. You could always hit a bog hole, I suppose."

"What will it cost?"

"Probably $2.00 or $2.50 for the wagon. Maybe cheaper when the water's low. If it weren't for the bramble along the river, this land would be mighty good for grazin' right here."

"How many head would you suppose it could support?" Tracker asked.

"Depends on how long you leave 'em, I reckon." Tap nodded. "They say it held ten thousand Indians and three hundred troops for a month."

√√"Ten thousand? When was that? We're not up near the Little Big Horn, are we?" Cabe quizzed.

"Nope. That's up past the Montana border. In '51 they moved the Ft. Laramie Treaty Council from the Fort to right here at the head of Horse Creek. Ten thousand Sioux, Cheyennes, Arapahos, Crows, and Snakes gathered with a few government officials and about three hundred troops for a big powwow."

Jacob Tracker pulled off his hat and wiped his brow. "Must have been quite a sight."

"You said it!" Tap nodded.

Tracker, how come the top of your forehead isn't lily-white like ever' cowman I've ever known? No one works outside without a hat except for prisoners.

"Is that another creek leadin' northeast?" Tracker pointed across the river.

"I think it's Spring Crick . . . but I'm not sure. You thinkin' of lookin' for a place around here?" Tap queried.

"Nope. It's too open." Tracker seemed to be searching for words. "Not enough protection from cold winds, storms, and all that. You know what I mean?"

Tap shoved his rifle, which had been draped across his lap, back into the scabbard as he stared at Jacob Tracker.

Too open for what? Why is it I keep thinkin' I'm not in on the whole plan here?

"Andrews," Cabe began, "you sure did drop that bushwhacker in a hurry. I thought you said they were friends of yours."

"Nope. They said they were friends. I only said I knew them. If you give me the choice between gettin' killed or shootin' back, I'll shoot back ever' time, no matter who's holdin' the gun. I figure the Lord's got my days numbered, but I don't want any dimwit with a gun tryin' to short-change me."

"Then how do me and Tracker know you won't be takin' a shot at us? You plannin' on shootin' me?" Cabe challenged.

"If I felt my life was in danger, I wouldn't give it a second thought. Boot Hill is full of men who waited too long. Take old Texas Jay back there. He was plannin' on sneakin' up behind and shootin' me in the back. But he was nervous and didn't sneak up nearly close enough. As soon as I whirled around and threw my rifle to my shoul-

94

der, it gave him a second thought about the matter. When he finally decided to go ahead and pull the trigger, he felt he had to hurry his shot and pulled it to the left."

"Well, I ain't the type to give it a second thought neither," Cabe insisted. "If I get the first shot, you're a dead man."

"It'll be a cold day in hades when you get the drop on me." Tap felt his face flush red. "You've got a .45 on you. Go for it!"

"Oh, I'll do it, Andrews. But I'll do it my way."

"Whoa!" Tracker intervened. "You're both on the same side this time. Let's ride up to the store and grab ourselves a stiff drink. Andrews, you figure on campin' in the willows tonight?"

"Nope. That would be like settin' bandit bait in those thickets, if you catch my drift. I'd like to cross the river and camp up against the hills," Andrews replied. "Besides, I never like puttin' off a river crossin'."

"Well, at least we can stop long enough to have that shot of whiskey," Cabe put in.

"You boys get what you need. I don't drink. Think I'll check out the dry goods."

"I've never met a shootist who didn't drink," Cabe blurted out.

"Well, you probably never met one that went to church either. You ever met an old gun-fighter?" Andrews pressed.

"No. Don't reckon so."

"I aim to be the first. Besides, I'm not a shootist anymore. I'm a brand inspector."

"Yeah, and I'm a lawyer," Cabe scoffed.

The store at Shaver's Crossing had at one time been an important stop on the Oregon Trail. Thousands of immigrant wagons had crossed the North Platte there, years before a bridge spanned the river near Ft. Laramie. The transcontinental railroad all but eliminated the need for wagons west, and by 1883 Shaver's was not much more than a crumbling log cabin saloon with one wall of mostly overpriced and outdated dry goods.

Four bored horses stood tied to a rail outside the front of the store. An old farm wagon with two black horses still hitched stood abandoned askew in the box elders near the river. The gray brush corrals behind the building held two mules, a tall swayback mare, and three weeks' worth of unshoveled manure. Several log rounds lounged across the front porch, waiting to be used for temporary seating.

The two windows in the front of the building were boarded up, giving the impression that the place was permanently closed. Scrawled in faded red paint on one of the boards were the words, "This saloon is open." The sign on the other boarded window was equally rustic. "Goods in Endless Variety." Two razor-thin dogs fought with a half-grown hog over the garbage that had been tossed out into the front yard.

Tracker pulled the buckboard over by the trees and at once got into some sort of argument with Cabe. Tap ignored them and tied Roundhouse

96

up next to a black gelding that was losing a battle with a swarm of gnats around his eyes. Swatting two mosquitos off the back of his hand and sucking in a big breath of musty stench, Andrews entered the dimly lit building.

An emotionless card game occupied four expressionless men with grimy hats and worn-out faces. At the bar a short man with a round hat stared into a shot glass devoid of whiskey. Tap couldn't tell if he was asleep or dead. He certainly wasn't moving. The other man at the bar waved his hands with every word he spoke, but no one listened.

Tap sauntered over to the bartender.

"That old boy talk his partner to death or what?" Tap grinned.

"He's been goin' on like that since this mornin'. Don't pay him no mind. He thinks he's King Frederick. Whatever you do, don't buy him a drink. We'll never get him to leave. What can I get you, mister?"

"I was hopin' for a good cup of coffee and a look at your dry goods."

"Dry goods? I'll sell you the whole store if you're interested. I'll get you some coffee, but I'll tell you the gospel truth — it ain't worth drinkin' except if you're half-asleep or full-drunk."

The man worked a wad of tobacco from between his teeth and spat it toward the floor behind the bar.

"Anything in particular you lookin' fer in dry

goods? Got some mighty fine canvas britches from San Francisco. Mr. Strauss makes a superior pair of overall jeans."

Tap took the tin cup of lukewarm coffee and swished it around to see how many grounds were floating in it. One swig of bitter, gritty brew caused him to shove his hat back and shudder. "Actually I was lookin' for some baby clothes. You don't happen to have anything like that, do you?"

The bartender, who wore an extremely well-used brown leather vest over his long-sleeved tan cotton shirt, pointed toward a trunk in the corner. "Baby clothes? That whole trunk is full of baby clothes. It was sittin' right there when I bought the store seven years ago. It ain't moved, and I ain't sold nothin' out of it. I'll sell you the trunk and ever'thing in it for five cash dollars."

"Let me take a look." Tap nodded. "The wife's expectin', and it would be nice to help her out with some new goods."

"I didn't say they was new. I think some pilgrim traded it for a ferry crossin' years ago. It's all used, but it's folded in there neat enough."

"Well, if you don't mind, I'd like to sort through it."

"Help yourself. Remember, the whole batch goes for five dollars. You do have that much cash on you, don't you?"

Tap glanced at the card game and back at the two men at the bar. Resting his right hand on the grip of his .44 Colt, he stared at the man. "Do you?"

"Do I what?" the bartender asked.

"Do you have five cash dollars in that cigar box under the bar?"

The man ran the back of his hand across his mouth. His eyes narrowed as he glared at Tap. "What I got or ain't got in my poke is none of your blasted business."

"Now, partner, I couldn't agree with you more. I surely don't need to know what's in your poke, and you don't need to know what's in mine. If I don't die from drinkin' the coffee, I'll sort through that trunk now."

He found the clothes moth-eaten and musty but neatly folded. He was about to close the trunk when Tracker and Cabe pushed their way into the building. From the far corner of the room, Tap watched as they strolled over to the bar.

You boys playin' cards seem mighty interested in those two. You don't happen to be plottin' some corrupt scheme, are you?

The mumbling man at the bar continued to blab.

The slumbering man slept on.

Two of the men at the card table quietly shoved their chairs back and rested their hands on the grips of their holstered revolvers.

A bearded man at the table reached into his vest pocket and pulled out a gold watch. He loosened his tie, and Tap could see that he had

99

perspired through his white shirt.

Andrews hunkered down behind the open trunk as if checking out the goods. He couldn't hear what Tracker and Cabe were saying, but he figured they must have ordered something because the bartender set an amber bottle and two glasses in front of them.

"You fellas passin' through?"

Tracker said something, but Tap could only hear the bartender's reply. "Lookin' fer work, are ya?"

Again there was some response that Tap couldn't hear.

"Well, that's good, 'cause there ain't much work around here."

The bartender continued to nod his head as Tracker and Cabe talked.

"You don't say! Goin' to buy a ranch, huh? Well, this side of the river Swan Land and Cattle's got about ever'thing tied up. They tell me he's runnin' almost 100,000 head of beef."

The bartender pulled a ragged hunk of tobacco out of his vest pocket, ripped off a piece of it with his teeth, and then offered the rest to the other two. Both quickly declined.

" 'Course, you'd have to go all the way to Custer City or back to Cheyenne to draw a bank draft. Unless you was carryin' a big poke with you. But that surely ain't none of my business."

Even from across the room, Tap could see Cabe reach for his vest pocket and then quickly put his hand back down.

That-a-boy, Wes, tell 'em where you keep your poke. Surely you two can tell when you're gettin' set up. A professional gambler wouldn't fall for that, would he? At least, not a successful one.

Tap could feel the sweat begin to roll down the back of his neck. There seemed to be absolutely no air circulation in the room. The man with the beard nodded, and two of the men at the table stepped lightly back toward the front door. Rather than exit, they loitered as if looking at a barrel of hard tack that was gathering dust by the entrance.

Makes a man wish he had a Greener. A snubnosed shotgun would cover ground a whole lot quicker. Now don't do anything dumb, boys. I've done enough shootin' for one day.

The man with the beard nodded his head at the bartender, who looked over at the babbling fool and cleared his throat. Suddenly the talking man shut up. Tracker and Cabe glanced his way.

Tap watched from behind the trunk lid as the man he thought was asleep hoisted Cabe's revolver and cocked the hammer. Cabe and Tracker spun around at the sound of the .45. The formerly blabbing drunk shoved a knife blade under Tracker's chin.

"What the . . . ," Cabe blustered.

The bearded man at the table nodded at the bartender, who looked at Tracker.

"You just put your pokes right out here on the table, and we might let you ride away." His smile showed heavily yellowed teeth.

"You can't do this!" Tracker complained.

"We can and we will!" the man holding the knife insisted. "You're dealin' with the Platte River Boys, mister. This is our territory, and it's goin' to cost you."

"Whatever you got ain't worth your life, now is it?" the man with Cabe's gun put in. "Either give us your goods, or we can just shoot ya and take it off ya! Don't make no difference to us."

Tracker's eyes searched the room. Andrews purposely kept out of sight behind the trunk.

"We got two at the table and two at the door. You ain't goin' nowhere," the bartender insisted. "Now where's the money? Are we goin' to take it dead or alive?"

"You aren't goin' to take it at all," Tap hollered as he stood up from behind the large trunk, his .44 cocked and aimed straight at the head of the bearded man. "Tell the two at the door to keep their guns in their holsters or you're a dead man, mister!"

The man waved his hands at the two at the door, and they stood still, hands still wide of their holsters.

"You cain't take on seven men, mister!" the one with the knife to Tracker's throat hollered.

"I just did."

"We'll kill ya. You won't get out of this," the bartender insisted.

"But at what cost?"

"I can slice this man's throat in a flash," the drunk said.

"You do and your boss over here at the table is dead."

"You ain't that good of a shot."

"The bullet will enter his head about halfway between his hat and his left eye," Tap asserted.

"But this here man will be dead."

"And the other one, too," the man with the gun on Cabe added.

"That might be," Tap responded. "My second shot will hit the big man at the door in the belly. I'll need to shoot fast, and I want a target I can't miss."

"You're crazy," the formerly sleeping drunk challenged. "We'll gun you down before you get to the door."

"Maybe, but two of you will be dead. And I'm mighty sure I can kill another and maybe sink lead into two more before I cross that last divide. You've got to figure out if all this is worth it."

"How do we know you're that good a shot?" the bearded man demanded.

"Ask Texas Jay. But he won't say much 'cause he's laying dead on the prairie."

"You killed Texas Jay?"

"With a shot about halfway between the brim of his hat and his left eye," Tap barked. "Now let those two go right now!"

"We ain't goin' to do it!"

"Well, then kill them!"

"What?" Cabe shouted.

Tap never took his aim off the bearded man at the table." Kill 'em so I can pull this trigger and send your boss to his just deserts."

"Wait!" the bearded man called. "Whatever's in that poke isn't worth anyone dyin' for, boys. Turn them loose."

"Now!" Tap hollered.

"Turn 'em loose," the boss insisted. "There's other ways to lift a poke."

"Just slide that revolver back into Cabe's holster," Tap commanded. "Tracker, you and Cabe roll the buckboard out onto the ferry. We're crossin' right now."

"You ain't leavin' alive," the big man at the door announced.

"Of course I am. Now you two get your tails over by the bar."

The bearded man at the table motioned for them to do just that.

Tap scooted toward the door, his right hand still gripping the pointed .44.

"We'll track you down and kill ya, mister!" one of the men hissed as he backed toward the bar.

"Maybe . . . maybe not. But I'll tell you something that will happen for sure. I'm goin' to shoot the first one who comes out this door."

"You ain't scarin' us none."

"I don't care if I'm scarin' you or not. Some in this room would probably like to live to see another day, and I'm just givin' you fair warnin'. Whoever steps out of that doorway before we cross the river will be shot on sight."

The bartender plastered the wooden floor with

another wad of tobacco juice. "You cain't hit the side of this building from the river."

"You know, that's the same thing those three old boys rustlin' sixty-four head of TS beef must have thought. They jumped me from two hundred yards away. I suppose you heard what happened to them."

"They was shot between their eyeballs and the brims of their hats," one man muttered.

The biggest of the bunch wiped his hand across his mouth. "You did that?"

The man with the beard continued to sit at the table littered with poker chips and cards. "How do we know he ain't bluffin', boys?"

"There's only one way to find out," Tap offered. "Just have a volunteer step out on that porch. How about it, boys? I figure the boss over there in that captain's chair ought to be the one. He seems to have the most doubts about my ability."

"You don't just ride away from the Platte River Boys!" The bartender smirked. "You better be watchin' your backside, mister!"

"It's a cinch you wouldn't have the guts to come straight at me, isn't it?"

Tap backed out through the doorway, closing the heavy wooden door as he went. He limped over to Roundhouse but kept his Colt on the door until he could pull the '73 out of the scabbard.

With the gun cocked and the long-range sight flipped up, he unhitched Roundhouse. Walking toward the river crossing, he kept the horse between him and the building.

Tracker and Cabe had the buckboard loaded on the steam-driven ferry that was no more than a large, flat raft hooked to cables. Cabe held a gun to the ferryman's back and got the craft moving the second Tap walked Roundhouse onto the rough-sawed wooden planks that served as flooring. With the gun at his shoulder, Tap continued to wait for someone to exit the building.

"I can't believe no one followed you," Tracker commented.

"I guess they believed the bluff. They're smarter than they look."

"Thanks for bailin' us out," Tracker added.

"Not that we couldn't have taken care of it ourselves," Cabe assured them.

Jacob Tracker looked over at him and shook his head. "Don't be stupid, Wes. We were about to be robbed and shot dead."

"I say I could have handled it!" Cabe yelled. "They weren't goin' to shoot nobody. It was all a bluff. I ain't thankin' no one."

"Well, I'm sorry I interfered with your plans. I was just watchin' your backside, and that's what you hired me to do. If I had already received my funds, I could have just let them plug you. When we head back, I suggest we stay on the Deadwood Road and cross at Ft. Laramie. These are hide-in-the-bushes-and-shoot-you-in-the-back boys around here."

"Anyone runnin' cattle out this way is goin' to have to put up with the likes of that mob. Why don't the authorities do something about the horse thieves and robbers along the river?"

"Well, this part of the county has only one deputy. He doesn't want to take them all on by himself. But if you're going to drive cattle up here from Pine Bluffs, it could be a problem."

"That's exactly why I needed to ride this trail. I want to know what I'm gettin' into. You reckon they'll follow us?" Tracker quizzed as the ferryman brought them to the other side.

"Maybe. That's why we're not goin' to let this ferryman know which direction we're headed." He turned to the older man in the tattered navy blue captain's hat. "What's it cost to ferry a wagon and a horse?"

The old man spat a chaw of tobacco far out into the river. His stained gray long-handled shirt looked like it hadn't been washed in a year. "At gunpoint?" he cackled.

"Regular."

"It's $2.50 for the wagon, $1.00 for the horse and rider."

"He's right," Tap replied. "A man shouldn't have to ride his own ferry at gunpoint. Give him $5.00, Cabe. It will be a bonus."

"What? We don't have to —"

"Sure we do. He did a good job under adverse conditions. He deserves to be paid well."

Tracker nodded, and Cabe dug out some money.

"You ain't goin' to shoot me when my back is turned, are you?" the old man asked.

"Nope."

"Well, I'm obliged to ya fer bein' generous. I surmised I was doin' this for free, and now I get extree. Yes, sir, the day's turnin' out better than I reckoned."

It was strictly a defensive camp.

Riding west until dark, Tap turned them north up Rawhide Creek and into the rolling hills. Their buckboard narrowed the choices of flight and completely eliminated any chance of stealing away undetected.

After watering the horses in the creek, they drove the wagon by moonlight to the mouth of a steep little coulee and parked it across the entrance. The horses were picketed behind the wagon in the protection of the gulch. Tap left his saddle on Roundhouse but pulled off the bridle.

He now sat cross-legged in the back of the buckboard staring out into the night. The other two stretched out under the wagon, but he knew they were awake. He could smell the aroma of their cheroots.

The moon was three-quarters full and perched slightly to the southwest. The stars seemed blasted into the sky like unfading Fourth of July fireworks. A whining chorus of cries from a coyote family drifted by like a memory that won't settle down. Tap hung his dusty black felt hat on the brake handle of the wagon.

Shoot the hat, boys.

Hot.

Dry.

Dark shadows.

He wiped his forehead with his bandanna, then retied it, letting it droop deep on his chest away from his neck. Tap unrolled a leather pouch, and even in the dark he found the small, thick glass bottle and a square patch of cloth. Opening the sliding gate on the rear of his Winchester, he pulled out the cleaning rod and began to screw the sections together.

Cleaning and oiling his guns was something Tap could do in the dark — with his eyes closed . . . half-asleep.

His hands continued the cleaning.

His eyes stared straight out into the night.

If that Platte River gang was goin' to jump us, it would be at night. Or from behind. We won't see them in daylight. They've got to be cleaned out, Lord. All those rustlers and thieves in the coulees and brush have got to be driven out of this country, or it will never settle down.

But I'm not the one. I've got a wife . . . a baby comin'. It's not my job, Lord. I can't go on livin' by the gun. Some parts of the country are settlin' down. Maybe I should just pack up Pepper and Angelita and move us to . . . to California. We could buy ourselves a little place along the foothills . . . maybe Sonora . . . Grass Valley . . . Placerville. Raise some beef to sell to the miners, plant a garden, braid a few reatas, *peddle hackamores and* mecates, *sit in the shade of big valley oak and watch the kids grow.*

The distant whine of the coyotes ceased. Tap looked more intently out into the darkness. He laid aside the cleaning rod, slowly cocked the lever of the rifle, and then put the gun to his shoulder. A horse whinnied behind him. He hunkered down in the wagon to make sure there was no silhouette.

He waited for a twig to snap.

A glow of a quirley.

A clomp of a hoof.

A signal whistle.

Shadowy movement.

Anything.

There was nothing.

It seemed like half an hour, but he knew it was more like five minutes when he finally sat back up, released the hammer of the rifle back down to a safety position, and reached over for his leather-wrapped canteen. The swig of water was tepid, slightly alkaline. He leaned his head over and poured some down the back of his neck. It felt cool running down his back and dripping on his chest. His shirt clung to his body.

Either no one's out there or it's Indians. That bunch at the crossing couldn't sneak that well.

The next six hours he spent dozing in and out of dreams about ranches in green rolling hills, babies crying all night, and coyotes howling at the moon.

At the first break of daylight, Tap fell out of the buckboard. He hadn't planned on tumbling to the dirt.

Cabe vaulted out of his bedroll and began firing his .45 randomly at the creek. "They killed Andrews!" he shouted.

Tap could hear the lever of Tracker's carbine cock. Still lying flat in the dirt to avoid Cabe's wild shooting, Tap hollered, "Put the guns down, boys. I didn't get shot. I just fell out of the wagon. I sat cross-legged most of the night, and my injured left leg lost all feeling. It collapsed the minute I put weight on it."

With one hand on a spoke of the wagon wheel, Tap pulled himself to his feet and brushed the dirt off his stiff light brown canvas britches.

Later, sitting around a breakfast fire, he tried pulling off his stove-top black boot. His left foot had swelled so much that the boot wouldn't budge.

"You think they'll be followin' us today?" Tracker asked him over a blue tin cup of steaming coffee.

"No. They aren't a daylight bunch. And they don't seem too anxious to face three guns. I figure they'll look for something easier."

Tap scraped his knife across the plate of beans and dunked his last bite of hard bread into his coffee before plopping it in his mouth. The lump scalded his throat as it went down.

"If you boys don't mind, I'd like to ride the wagon this mornin' and keep my foot up. It swelled to where I can't pull off my boot."

"You figure that leg's busted?" Tracker asked. "Maybe you ought to ride up to Ft. Laramie and see a doctor."

"I knew a gambler in Tucson by the name of Nacemiento who fell out of a two-story window and busted his leg. Got gangrene and died within two months," Cabe added.

Tap glanced over at him and shook his head. "You always this cheerful?"

They rolled out of camp about the time the sun was a huge orange ball above the distant Sand Hills of Nebraska. They creaked and bounced their way to the east of Rawhide Mountain, up Red Cloud Slew, which was as parched as the prairie itself, and on across the uninterrupted dry grasslands that sloped gently down toward the Leau Qui Court River.

A little after noon Tap was able to pull off his boot and examine his throbbing leg. From above his knee to his toes was one continuous bruise. Not wanting his foot to swell so large he couldn't wear his boot, he shoved the dirty sock-covered foot back into the stiff leather and painfully yanked the boot back in place.

Tracker turned the wagon toward the setting sun. Right before dark they rolled into the Deadwood-Cheyenne stage stop at Running Water. It was no more than a huge stone barn and two unpainted wood-frame buildings surrounded by a couple dozen hurriedly pitched tents. One building served as housing, the other as a roadhouse cafe and saloon. The barn had originally served as a fortress for man and beasts against attacks from the Sioux and northern Cheyenne. Now it marked the campsite of dozens of prospectors digging for color on Silver Cliff.

"Figured it's about time we ate somethin' besides our own cookin'," Tracker explained as he parked the wagon next to the stone barn. "Looks like we can camp out anywhere they aren't diggin' for gold."

He and Cabe brushed the road dust off their hats and headed for the cafe. Tap stayed back to water Roundhouse.

"Well, ol' boy, you had a day off. My foot's feelin' a little better, and the evenin's dry and hot. Summertime in the northern range . . . a big ol' boy like you probably has never been south of Denver."

Tap brushed the horse down with a folded saddle blanket.

"You'd look mighty fine in Santa Fe with some well-dressed señorita sitting sidesaddle on you paradin' around the plaza. Yes, sir . . . providin' you didn't dump her on those fancy Spanish combs."

Roundhouse tugged at the lead rope when Tap began to smooth the saddle blanket on the horse's back.

"Now I know what you're thinkin'. It's about dark. Day's over. Surely you won't have to do night work. Let me tell you somethin'. I've spent a lifetime going into dives like this one. Ever' once in a while I have to leave in a hurry, and I don't intend on tryin' to ride you bareback. So I'll just leave you in the ready position."

Tap jerked the latigo tight and tied it around the saddle's d-ring. The horse whipped his head around as if to bite. Andrews gently popped his clenched left fist into the horse's nose, and Roundhouse immediately twisted his head back straight.

Retrieving a small grain sack out of the back of the buckboard, Tap scooped up a handful of rolled oats.

"Take it easy, boy. You're feedin' the mice with most of that. . . . You can just take a little snooze here at the rail. We'll go make camp in an hour or so, I suppose."

He tied the horse at the right end of the rail next to the corral. It wasn't the closest position to the building, but it was the easiest one from which to mount a horse on the off side.

The inside of the cafe was crammed with people, conversation, and smoke.

Bummers on their way to the Black Hills.

Grubby prospectors who believed their fortune was only six feet of hard rock away.

Drovers looking for day work between the spring and fall roundups.

Drummers headed for Deadwood or Cheyenne.

Gamblers with dull white shirts and sweaty starched collars.

Freighters . . . drifters . . . railroad surveyors.

Tracker and Cabe were in an animated conversation with a tall, thin man at a bar that looked as if it had been attacked with an axe and then repaired with rough-cut 2 x 4s.

A group of men stood around a table perched under a bright kerosene lamp.

It's either a mighty interesting card game or the one thing this place is missing.

A well-dressed woman sat at the table trying to eat supper while a dozen men huddled like buzzards around her. She was the only woman in the room. The man beside her was tackling a chop about the size of a small hog and seemed indifferent to the interest his companion was stirring.

Dressed in a long-sleeved royal blue velvet dress, offset by black lace located in provocative places, she would have undoubtedly drawn a suspicious glance in most civilized companies — which this was not.

Her jet-black hair was pulled up behind her head in ivory combs, and she exuded a stately, cultured air. She glanced up as Tap stepped closer. Their eyes met through the crowd.

"Mr. Andrews! I'm surprised to see you alive. I certainly thought that blonde-headed bobcat would have stabbed you in the back and stole all your money by now!"

"Selena, it's good to see you haven't lost any of your charms! Do you still carry that sneak gun in your belt?"

Several of the men began to back away from

her table. Tap pushed his hat back and stepped up in the gap they left.

"Yes, and I still have that long Mexican dagger in my sleeve," she smiled, "in case you were planning on trying something."

The last of the crowd of men filtered back across the room.

"Come sit down and have supper with us." She motioned. "You've chased off all the other men. You'll have to tell me how Pepper's getting along. Have you seen Stack lately? You heard about Danny Mae and Wiley, didn't you?"

The slightly graying, stocky man with gravy on his chin and puzzlement in his eyes looked up from his plate of food to stare at Tap.

"This is my, eh . . . this is Mr. Colton Banner." She turned to wave her bejeweled right hand. "And this is Mr. Tapadera Andrews. He shoots people for a living. He's very good at it."

5

The red brick Union Pacific train depot in Cheyenne felt both foreign and familiar. Five months earlier it had been the stage for a deadly shootout when Alex Del Gatto and gang attempted to rob two treasure-laden trains at the same time. Deputies Tapadera Andrews and Carbine Williams and Andrews's wife had sent most of the leaders of the gang to face their final divine judgment.

Now Pepper and Angelita sat in the very same lobby waiting to transfer onto the Colorado Central for a trip south to Boulder. The crowd in the terminal ignored the obviously pregnant blonde woman and her brown-skinned, dark-haired companion, much to Pepper's relief. The aroma of fresh bread blended with the smell of cigar smoke and new leather. Under the chattering din of the crowd, the two conversed in privacy as they sat on a hard wooden bench along the red-bricked east wall.

"Do you see anyone you know?" Pepper asked Angelita.

"You mean, besides Mr. Ferguson, the ticket agent?"

"Yes. I don't recognize any of these passengers. We haven't been away from Cheyenne that long, have we?"

"Lots of people pass through here that never stick around. You know what I mean? Do I have to wear this?" Angelita tugged at the small yellow straw hat held in place by a white lace ribbon tied under her chin.

"Yes. A lady should wear a hat when she travels."

"But I'm not a lady — yet."

"Think of this as school. You're training to be a lady."

"Why?"

"Why what?"

Angelita swung her high-top black lace-up shoes back and forth as she sat on the tall bench. "Why do I want to be a lady?"

"Because that's what God expects of us. Besides, true gentlemen will take an interest in you if you know how to be a lady."

"Is Mr. Andrews a true gentleman?"

Pepper took a big sigh and tried to brush down the front of her light blue dress before she realized that the bulge she fussed with was her stomach. "Mr. Andrews is trying very hard to learn how to be a gentleman. Things like being a lady and a gentleman are easier learned when you are young. That's why I want you to keep trying."

"When I get big, I think I'll marry someone like Mr. Andrews. Only my husband has to own a gold mine." A small boy in a tight white shirt and a tie sat on a bench staring at her. Suddenly Angelita stuck out her tongue. The boy blushed red and looked away at the front door.

"What do you like about Mr. Andrews?" Pepper asked.

118

"Well . . . he's strong, and he knows how to take care of you, and he never gets scared; he works hard; he goes to church with you; he doesn't come home drunk; he doesn't chew tobacco, and he needs you to take care of him."

"Those are good qualities."

"You know," Angelita continued, "he's not bad-looking, even for an older man. Oh, but don't tell him I said that. You know, the part about not being bad-looking."

Pepper threw back her head and laughed.

"Did I say something funny? What did I say?"

"What you said was delightful." Pepper giggled. "And I can't promise I won't tell Mr. Andrews. You're a very insightful young lady."

"Is that good?"

"Yes. It means you take time and think things through. I like that."

"Do you know what I've been thinking through a lot in the past few minutes?"

"No. What?"

"I've been wondering if you have any blank paper, a bottle of ink, and a pen," Angelita replied.

Pepper glanced down at her valise. "No. Why? Did you want to write a letter?"

"Oh, not exactly. I was just thinking . . ."

"Thinking about the old days? Angelita Gomez, you are not going to peddle phony autographs!"

"Pepper Andrews!" The voice sounded musical and loud but on tune, almost haunting.

Searching toward the door of the train depot, she spied a familiar well-dressed form.

"Savannah!" Pepper struggled to her feet and waded through the crowd, Angelita at her side. Halfway across the room, she noticed a nobby-dressed man with round derby hat and large mustache standing at Savannah's side. His white shirt was starched, his tie was silk, and the badge on his chest was shiny silver and read U.S. Marshal.

"Now look at you," Savannah purred. "You're beginning to look like a mama!"

"I'm fat, Savannah. Just plain fat."

"Nonsense. You look delightful — in a womanly way. Pepper, this is my fiancé, Marshal Tobert C. Stillwell."

He took off his hat. Gray streaked the thick, wavy dark brown hair. He gently shook her hand.

"Toby, this is a very dear friend, Mrs. Pepper Andrews."

"Mighty pleased to meet you, ma'am. Is your husband with you? I'd like to talk to him. I've heard a lot about how he cleaned the riffraff out of Cheyenne after Pappy was killed."

"I'm afraid Tap's up north chasin' cows. He's working as brand inspector now."

"Sure like to talk him into comin' down to the Indian Nation and helpin' me out," the big man boomed.

"Eh, uh hem!"

"Oh, excuse me," Pepper apologized. "Savannah, you remember Baltimore's daughter Angelita?"

"Why, yes. How's your father, dear?"

"He continues to make slow progress with his afflictions, but with the help of the Almighty, we believe he will fully recover."

"Those are big words from a little lady." The marshal smiled.

"Angelita is a special, dear friend of ours." Pepper slipped her arm around the girl's shoulders.

"I can see that." Stillwell nodded. "If you ladies will excuse me, I'd like to borrow a sheet of paper and jot a note to Mr. Andrews. I was serious about the offer. I'd like you to carry a letter for me."

"I'll be happy to," Pepper smiled, "but Tap's retired from the lawman business."

"Think I'll write to him anyway. Perhaps he could recommend some men with sand."

Pepper followed Savannah across the depot. *She always manages to look like a queen entering her court no matter where she goes.*

Sitting on a hard, polished bench, Savannah spread her flowing violet dress and beckoned Pepper and Angelita to join her.

"I know, I know what you're going to say. Why on earth would I want to marry another lawman?"

"Well, it did cross my mind." Pepper folded her hands on her lap and tried not to think about how plain . . . and fruitful she must look next to Savannah.

"It's my calling. It's what I do best. The Lord

knows I didn't go looking for another lawman. In fact, when I came back west after visiting family in Charleston, I was determined not to marry again. But there I was at a hotel in Ft. Smith, and Toby was sitting alone eating supper. The waitress said he'd been eating alone for years, ever since his wife was killed by bandits out in the Indian Nation. Well, I thought to myself, *Poor man — he'd probably like someone to talk to*. Then," Savannah raised her eyebrows, "one thing led to another."

"I bet it did!" Pepper shook her head.

"We're going to wait until next spring to get married. He's a good Christian man, you know," Savannah explained.

"You've convinced me." Pepper grinned. "And you have my blessings and prayers."

"Thank you, dear. In a world of many shallow friendships, yours is one of the most genuine I have. Now if I were you, I wouldn't let Tap even see that letter. The Nation is no place for a lawman at the present time. Toby's the boss. He can sit in Ft. Smith and do the paperwork. But the deputies follow some extremely dangerous trails."

"Tap's enjoying the slower pace of being a brand inspector."

"Yes," Angelita added, "he only had to shoot dead three men the other day."

"Oh, my!" Savannah's astonishment sounded more routine than sincere.

"It's not all that dangerous — usually." Pepper's tone was flat and emotionless.

"I am one lady you don't have to explain it to," Savannah assured her. "If you think about how much danger they're in, it will drive you mad."

"Here comes our train!" Angelita jumped to her feet and ran to the big window.

"You will write to me about the baby, won't you?" Savannah insisted.

"Yes, you'll receive an announcement."

"And so will you — for the wedding. Make sure you enjoy each good day the Lord gives you, Pepper. Oh, you'll have some tough ones come along, but the joy of the good ones will see you through. Believe me, I speak from a deep well of experience."

Pepper stood up, carrying her small green valise. Her eyes met Savannah's and for a minute locked.

"I'll miss you, Savannah Divide," Pepper finally murmured.

"And I, you, Pepper Andrews."

Pepper leaned over carefully and gave Savannah a gentle hug. Then she turned around to face the kind, soft eyes of Marshal Stillwell. He tipped his hat and handed her a folded letter.

"Nice to meet you, ma'am."

Pepper took the letter. "You know you're taking the sunlight away from Cheyenne, don't you?"

He glanced over at Savannah. "Yes, ma'am, I believe I do. But I figure the Lord's blessings are meant to be shared. It's Ft. Smith's time for some radiance."

"You might be right, Marshal. Take care of her — she's a special lady."

"Indeed she is, ma'am, indeed she is."

Angelita sat by the window, her little case in her lap. She studied the dry Colorado landscape. Pepper's eyes reflected the speeding images of brown grass and dark, distant mountains.

Lord, Savannah is always charming. Always full of grace. Always patient. I've tried and tried this year, but I can't seem to get very good at it. I still say dumb things. I worry. I fuss. I end up doing things I promised I would never do again. You must get very tired of my constant failings.

"Oh, look! Antelope!" Angelita shouted.

Pepper took a deep breath and sighed. Then she slipped her arm around Angelita's shoulder and peeked out the crowded passenger car window.

The Rocky Mountain Sanitarium was a two-story brick hospital located on the west side of Boulder, Colorado. Pepper and Angelita strolled to the Alexandria Hotel, left their bags in their room, and then hiked to the hospital along the tree-lined streets. The vast prairie stretched east from the city, and the continental divide defined the immediate west.

"It's not as hot as in Pine Bluffs," Angelita announced. "Do you think it's hot? Maybe we should slow down. Are you getting tired? If you want to stop and rest, that's all right with me. I can't believe we just up and decided to come visit Father. I didn't get to write and tell him we're coming. Did you know it's been ten weeks since I've seen him? Do you think I've changed any in the past ten weeks? I think I've changed quite a bit. I know I'm a little taller. I can mount Onespot without having to change the stirrups."

"I'd say you are quite nervous about seeing your father." Pepper reached over and took her hand as they continued to amble down the slightly warped wooden sidewalk. The dirt lane up to the sanitarium was lined with elm trees, green lawn, and patches of white and purple morning glory.

"It's beautiful here in the summer. I'm glad my father can be here, I mean if he has to be paralyzed."

"Perhaps he's better. We heard from Mr. Williams that he was able to wiggle some fingers and move his head and neck."

"Yes. I wish . . ." Angelita paused and looked down at her shoes.

"You wish what?"

"I wish he'd never gotten shot."

Pepper stopped and hugged Angelita. "I know, honey, that's what I wish, too."

"How come God let that happen?"

"Well, we live in a world where bad people do bad things."

"I wish we had a better world." Angelita sniffed.

"I think that's what heaven's all about."

Angelita turned back toward the front of the hospital. "I'll race you to the door!"

"What?"

"Oh . . . yeah. I guess a woman in your delicate condition can't run." Angelita chewed on her tongue and looked around the grounds. "Count and see how many seconds it takes me to run to the front door. Ready. Set. Go!"

Off she went. Her straw hat blew back and bobbed against her black pigtails. She held her dress far above her ankles, revealing black shoes, white socks, and brown-skinned legs.

One.

Lord.

Two.

She is such a delight.

Three.

One minute an inquiring young lady.

Four.

The next just a little child wanting to play.

Five.

But I've never seen . . .

Six.

. . . such a quick mind in any child.

Seven.

Of course, I've never really . . .

Eight.

. . . been around many children.

Nine.

Yet.

Ten.

Angelita trotted back, her hat still held to her back by the ribbon tied under her chin. "How many seconds? Huh? How fast was I?"

"I think it was just a tad over nine seconds."

"Wow! That's good, isn't it?" They approached the front door of the sanitarium. "Did I ever tell you about the time I outran nine boys?"

"You ran against the boys? What kind of race was that?"

"I didn't say it was a race. I stole their baseball, and they were all chasin' me. But they didn't catch me."

"I hope you gave them back their baseball."

"Yeah." She grinned as she held the door open for Pepper. "I sold it back to them for two bits."

Ward B was a room on the west side of the building on the first floor. It was about one hundred feet long and twenty-five feet wide. Beds were generously spaced on each side of the room, with white cloth dividers to give each patient a bit of privacy. Pepper noticed that only half the beds were occupied.

Light blazed into the room from the long vertical uncurtained windows that lined the west wall. The air was warm to the point of stuffy and heavy with the smell of cleaner. The wooden floor was worn but polished to a spotless shine. Muted voices could be heard throughout the room. A rather large woman shoved her way out through swinging doors at the far end of the room.

"Angelita-Bonita!" an unseen voice boomed

127

out as they proceeded toward the north end of the room.

"Daddy!" Angelita took off running around the partition separating the farthest bed from its neighbors.

Pepper stepped around the corner. Baltimore Gomez was strapped to a chair beside the bed, his feet resting on a small padded stool. He was neatly shaved and wore clean ducking trousers and a long-sleeved, three-button white cotton pullover shirt. His suspenders hung off the side of the chair; his feet were bare. Angelita had taken his left arm and draped it around her shoulder. His thick black hair, eyebrows, and mustache showed flecks of gray. His eyes sparked joy.

A tear slid down his face, but Angelita quickly wiped it away with the palm of her hand.

"Mrs. Andrews, you two ladies have made this a glorious day!" Baltimore exclaimed.

"Mr. Gomez, you are looking very good. Now how did you know it was Angelita walking across this room? There's no way to see her, with you behind the partition."

"Oh, there is a special music in my daughter's step — for me, it is a very familiar tune." He smiled. "I'm surely glad you came. I reckon I knew you would when you read my letter."

"What letter?" Angelita asked, still clinging to her father's arm.

"You didn't get my letter?" he asked.

Pepper pulled up a straight-back wooden chair

next to his and sat down. It was a relief to release her feet from the weight. "No. When did you mail it?"

"A couple weeks ago. Right after I heard that you moved back to Cheyenne."

"Moved?" Angelita queried. "We didn't move. We still live in Pine Bluffs."

"But Carbine came for a visit and said he heard the mayor say he was goin' to get Tap to move back to Cheyenne and take the marshal's job."

"No, we have no intention of going back."

"Well, no wonder you didn't get the letter. Oh, my little one." He squeezed Angelita's shoulder. "We have much to talk about."

"Baltimore," Pepper gasped, "you moved your arm!"

"Look!" he announced. "Look at this!" He raised his left arm high above his head, clenched his fist, and then opened it. Finally he lowered his arm, swung it around, and gave Angelita another hug. She wiped away two more tears from his cheeks and several from her own.

"Did you get dust in your eyes, Father? I believe I got some in mine," she explained.

"When did this happen?" Pepper asked.

"About a month ago I began to have some feeling in my arm. Then I could wiggle my fingers, move my wrist, and finally my whole arm. The doctors think it's a miracle."

"It is, Father. We pray for you every day."

He took a big, deep breath. This time Angelita just let the tears stream down his leather-tough brown cheeks. "And look. This week I have gained some feeling in my left foot as well. I can wiggle my toes. Watch me, watch . . . Do you see that?"

"That is wonderful, Baltimore!"

"Oh . . . but what about you? I got so excited with my Angelita here, I forgot. You look like a lady with a baby, if I could be so bold."

"I look like a lady with a very big baby! I am feeling very well, thank you. Your daughter is a great help to me. Tap and I feel very fortunate to have her stay with us."

"I've surely missed her," Baltimore admitted. "Well, if you two didn't get my message, why are you here?"

"Tap got a little job on the side. So he gave us train fare."

"What kind of job? Is he back to marshalin'?"

"No. He escorted a Texas rancher up to the Lightning Creek region. A Mr. Tracker, I think his name was. Anyway, Tracker wants to buy a ranch up there and paid Tap handsomely. Besides, Tap wanted to check on some cattle anyway."

"Tracker? I knew a Tracker in New Mexico. He was a horse thief and cattle rustler. Robbed a bank in Tres Casas and killed the owner."

"This man's name is Jacob Tracker, but I'm sure he isn't the same man."

"No, I don't reckon he is. That old boy couldn't last long at the rate he was goin'. He probably got hung by now."

"We didn't come here to talk about horse thieves," Angelita scolded.

"Yes, Miss Gomez, I'm sure you didn't. It must be divine providence that brought you here. I surely do have a lot to talk to you about."

The large woman who had exited the room earlier returned carrying a pitcher of water. Her round face was pretty, and Pepper was surprised at how graceful she seemed to be with ordinary chores.

"First off, let me introduce you to my nurse, Mrs. Baker." The full-figured woman smiled warmly. "And this is my darlin' daughter Angelita, who I've told you so much about."

"I'm so glad to meet you," the nurse replied. "Your father thinks the world of you, young lady."

"Yes, I know." Angelita beamed.

"And this is Mrs. Andrews." He nodded toward Pepper. "She and Mr. Andrews have been taking care of my Angelita."

"I think it is a very special thing you are doing, Mrs. Andrews."

"Please, Mrs. Baker, call me Pepper."

The big nurse poured Baltimore a glass of water and set the pitcher on a table near his bed. "Yes, and call me Posse."

"Posse?" Angelita gasped.

"Yes, isn't that a funny nickname? I bet you've never heard of a woman called Posse before."

Angelita stared wide-eyed at the nurse. "Mr. Andrews knew a lady named Posse once!"

131

"Well, there you have it — what a coincidence. I've never run across anyone with my name before, but I always said it would happen someday. Tell me, where did your husband meet such a lucky lady?"

"Oh . . . I, eh, he just . . ." Pepper stammered. "Well, actually he was telling us about a frigid cold winter up in Bodie when he and a couple gamblers shared a cabin with . . . well —"

"Andrews? Tap?" the woman almost shouted. "Your husband is Tapadera Andrews?"

Pepper felt very self-conscious as the woman looked her over.

"Balty, why on earth didn't you tell me your Angelita was staying with Tapadera Andrews?"

"Well, I didn't, eh, you, eh, I guess I never . . ."

"You really are Posse LaFayette?" Angelita asked.

"Used to be LaFayette. Before I got married."

"Then it's true that Mr. Andrews carried you out of that burning cabin?"

"Yes, he did. Saved my life more than once, he did."

More than once?

" 'Course, I looked different back then. I was just a little slip of a thing. That was before I had five kids."

"Five?" Pepper took a deep breath and for the first time in weeks felt rather slim.

"Yes, but my Leppy died last summer, and I've had to work. Candance McCuttle told me

Tap died in some Arizona prison. Did you ever know Candance?"

"Eh, no."

"Well, you've probably heard Tap talk about her."

"Not really."

"Never mind. Listen, I've got others to check in on. You all have a nice visit. I need to have a long talk with you, young lady." She addressed Angelita.

"You do?"

"You probably have a million questions to ask me," Posse suggested.

Angelita's bright brown eyes grew wide. "Why?"

"They didn't get the letter," Baltimore explained.

"But I mailed it myself," Posse insisted.

"Well, they didn't get it, and I've got a lot of explainin' to do."

"In that case, I'll definitely let you alone to visit." Posse flashed a relaxed smile of straight white teeth.

Pepper caught a flash in Baltimore's eyes.

The afternoon passed quickly with a running dialog between Baltimore, Angelita, Pepper, and Mrs. Posse Baker. The long summer twilight at the base of the Rockies had begun when the two visitors began their long walk back to the hotel. They held hands and strolled leisurely as they enjoyed a slight breeze that made the hot

July air more bearable.

"This has been quite an afternoon, young lady."

Angelita held her hat by the neck ribbon and twirled it around as she walked. "Did you ever have a time where it seemed like you were just standing back watching yourself? That's the way this afternoon has been. I didn't think my father would ever want to get married again."

"Mrs. Baker seems sincerely fond of your father and is willing to take care of him," Pepper commented.

"Can you imagine a stepmother named Posse?"

"Well, I've been called Pepper all my life. It's not all that different, is it?"

"Pepper is a great name. It means you're hot-headed and spicy!"

"It does?"

"That's what Mr. Andrews told me it meant."

"Oh, he did, did he?"

"But Posse means a whole bunch of men chasing a bad guy. What kind of name is that? My mother's name was Rachel."

"You could call her Mrs. Baker."

"If they get married, then I'd have to call her Mrs. Gomez. That's dumb."

"I suppose you could call her Mama. I'm sure that's what her children call her."

"She isn't my mother."

"She's a nice lady. And a hard-working woman. It's not easy for a woman to support five children."

"What's a *nymph du prairie?*" Angelita asked.

Pepper stopped walking and turned and looked at her. "What?"

"The other day Mr. Andrews said that when he knew Posse, she was one of those. Is that sort of like a dance-hall girl?"

Pepper breathed a deep sigh and tried to brush her blonde hair back behind her head. "Yes, I think you could say it's similar to a dance-hall girl in some ways."

"You used to be a dance-hall girl when you were younger, didn't you?"

"Eh, yes, I did. How do you know so much about my past?"

"Mr. Andrews told me."

"What else did he tell you about me?" Pepper quizzed.

"He says that you are the prettiest woman he ever met in his life and that his heart does a little jump every time he hears your voice."

"He told you that?"

Angelita skipped as Pepper walked. "Yeah. One time I asked him how to know which person to marry."

"When did you talk about that?"

"Last winter in Cheyenne. You know when that boy named Milford fell out of the wagon on his head and spent two weeks saying he wanted to marry me."

"I don't remember that. Whatever happened to Milford?"

"He got better."

"Well, your father is old enough to know what he's doing. He can't stay in the hospital much longer. The city of Cheyenne has set a limit as to how much financial help they can give him."

"I don't want to live with all those kids."

"But Posse's oldest daughter is just a year or so older than you. It might be nice to have a close friend."

"Did you ever have an older sister?"

"No," Pepper admitted.

"I don't want someone else telling me what to do."

"Your father said you could stay with us until school starts again."

"Do you think perhaps tomorrow I could come talk to my father alone?" Angelita asked.

"I think that's a very good idea."

"Without 'her' around either?"

"I'm sure that can be arranged."

"Good, because I've got a thing or two to tell him. You know," she said sighing, "sometimes a man needs a woman around to tell him what to do."

"I believe that's exactly what your father thinks also."

Supper at the Alexandria Hotel reminded Pepper more of McCurleys' Hotel than the Inter Ocean in Cheyenne. Big family-style tables. Piles of plain but very tasty food. Deep laughter. Active conversation.

Pepper and Angelita were busy talking to a

couple from England when a deep voice from somewhere behind her caused her to drop a fork in her china plate and spin around in the polished oak chair. The tall man at the door was dressed in a stiff white shirt and long black topcoat. He held a fine black beaver hat in his hand. With gold studs lining his shirt, he looked ready to attend the opera.

The square jaw.

The weathered lines flaring from the soft brown eyes that looked out under full, bushy eyebrows, the politeness in his tone, even though most would concede to him solely because of this strength.

"It's Stack!" she murmured to Angelita.

"Who?"

"A very good friend of ours. You've heard us mention his name."

"Oh, yes . . . Mr. Lowery. He's the one who visited us last May."

"Excuse me just a moment," Pepper requested of the couple sitting across from them. She stood just as the tall man's eyes met hers. An ear-to-ear smile swept over his face as he handed his hat to a waitress and waded through the crowd to reach her.

"Pepper darlin', how are you?" He started to hug her, then backed away.

"My-oh-my, it looks like you and that no-good Arizona gunslinger came through the winter well."

Pepper could feel her face blush.

"When's the glorious event?"

"It's still a couple months or so. I'm getting fat, Stack."

"It sure ain't like the last time."

Pepper drew a deep breath and let out a long sigh. "There is nothing about it that's like the last time. Praise the Lord."

"I can't believe I've found you here. Where is that Tapadera?" Stack searched the room with his eyes.

"He's up in Laramie County checking on cows. This is our good friend Angelita Gomez. You might know her father, Baltimore."

"Just a little."

"Well, he's recovering from a gunshot wound at the hospital here, and we took the train down to visit him. Now you've got to tell me about yourself. Last we heard you were freightin' up to the Black Hills. And here you are dressed for the theater."

"Ain't this somethin'? It's all kind of crazy, Miss Pepper. Did you ever have times that you just sort of stood back and watched yourself go through the motions?"

"I have!" Angelita called out.

"This is a long story, and I hardly believe it myself."

Pepper motioned to the empty chair beside her. "Sit down and join us for supper. I'd like to hear all about what caused Stack Lowery to dress up like he was attending a mine owners' convention."

Stack slipped down beside Pepper, careful not to crack his knees on the table. He nodded warmly at the couple across the table and then turned to Pepper. "Actually I'm in town attending a — you aren't goin' to believe this, Miss Pepper. I hardly believe it myself."

"What won't I believe?"

"I'm attending a mine owners' meeting."

"No, really, Stack . . . why are you —" Pepper stared at him with her mouth open. "You really are, aren't you?"

"Yep."

"What on earth would make you dress up like that and attend a mine owners' meeting? There isn't some pretty lady involved in this, is there?" she badgered.

Stack's face turned as red as a ripe watermelon as he watched a waitress pour him a steaming cup of coal-black coffee. She thought about all the times that she and the other girls at April Hasting's Dance Hall had relentlessly teased him about which woman he should marry.

"Ain't no lady . . . yet, Miss Pepper. But I've been givin' it some mighty serious thought."

"Oh?" Pepper raised her eyebrows and grinned. "Is this lady anyone I know?"

"No, no . . . I didn't mean I had one picked out. No, ma'am," he stammered, looking away from Pepper. "I've just been thinkin' that it's time, you know, for me to find myself a good woman and settle down."

"Don't look at me," Angelita blurted out. "My

father won't let me get married until I'm at least sixteen. Besides, I'm going to marry a man who owns a gold mine."

Stack stared at Angelita, looked back at Pepper, then back at Angelita. Suddenly a wide grin swept across his wide, friendly face. "Well, Miss Angelita, you certainly know how to break a man's heart."

"Yes, well, into every life comes occasional bitter disappointment." She nodded and jabbed her spoon into a large lump of brown gravy-laden mashed potatoes.

"So you're looking for a wife. I think that's great, Stack." Pepper reached over and put her hand on his arm. "But that still doesn't tell me what you're doing at a mine owners' meeting. Is there something you're ashamed to tell me?"

Again he blushed. "Well, I just ain't used to it yet, Miss Pepper. I know I look out of place."

"What is it that you're not used to?" she demanded.

"That I'm half owner of one of the largest gold mines in the Black Hills."

"You're what?" Pepper choked.

"You own a gold mine?" Angelita squealed. "Listen, I, eh, I might be able to talk my father into letting me get married at fifteen . . . really."

Pepper glared at Angelita.

"That was too obvious, wasn't it? I shouldn't have said that. I didn't mean it. Really, I'm just a kid."

"How old did you say she was?" Stack asked.

"Ten going on thirty. How in the world did you end up with a gold mine?"

"Half a gold mine."

"Tell me the whole story," Pepper demanded.

"You two go ahead and eat. I'll have them start cookin' my chop while I explain."

"Good. Now the last thing we knew, you were hauling freight between Cheyenne and the Black Hills."

"Yes, ma'am, that's right. My little sister's husband landed me a freightin' job, and it pays real good, too. I'd been savin' ever' penny all winter and spring and had come up with a tidy poke. You know, a little nest egg. Thought maybe I'd buy myself a store or something like that. Then I got to Deadwood about the first of June with two heavy wagons of cash-on-delivery mining equipment. Took me six extra days, the goin' was so slow.

"Well, I got to Pharaoh's Gulch, and a man by the name of Whip Bitters told me it all belonged to him, but he couldn't pay me. He wanted me to give him credit, and he'd give me half interest in this mine he was diggin'."

"He tried to stiff you?" Angelita broke in.

"One thing's for sure, he didn't have the money. He and two others was sleepin' out on the ground in front of the mine shaft hopin' to strike color. I couldn't imagine cartin' that gear back to Cheyenne, so I figured maybe the freight company would take the shares."

"And when you got back, they said the C.O.D.

was coming out of your poke?" Pepper guessed.

"Yes, ma'am. Took ever' penny I had saved for six months, plus I had to haul three loads for free. Well, I thought I would starve to death. But about the first of July, I was up in the Black Hills, and this Whip Bitters sent word for me to come see him at the Cosmo Hotel. When I went in, he was sittin' there dressed like a California banker."

"Like you are now?" Angelita asked.

"Yep. Well, Bitters was talkin' to some San Francisco men about selling the mine. He called it the Sphinx. He had struck a big vein at two hundred feet and was gettin' ready to sell out to these big shots. He told 'em I owned half interest, and they offered me $50,000 for my share."

"Wow, $50,000!" Angelita squealed, then put her hand over her mouth.

"That's wonderful, Stack! You'll be able to buy a store and everything!"

"You know," Angelita broke in, "I have very big feet."

Both Stack and Pepper stared at her.

"Don't I, Mrs. Andrews? Everyone says I have large feet, and that means I'll probably grow very tall. You know, by the time I'm sixteen." She glanced up to the glare of Pepper Andrews. "Eh, can I have some pie?"

"You may have some pie when you have finished eatin' everything on your plate."

"Even this slimy green stuff?"

"Yes, spinach will help you grow tall."

Angelita looked down at her plate. "Oh."

"So you sold your share for $50,000?" Pepper quizzed.

"Eh, no, ma'am. I, eh, well . . . I got to figurin', and, shoot, Miss Pepper, I kind of like the idea of being a gold mine owner. So I told them men I'd like to just let it ride."

"So you still own it?"

"Half of it."

"Well, is it paying off?"

"Four weeks ago they broke into a cavern the size of this room with gold flakes piled on the floor and hangin' from the ceilin'. For eight straight days they just scooped it up in gunny sacks and sent it direct to the smelter."

"Wow!" Angelita's eyes grew big. "Did you make more than $50,000?"

"Miss Angelita, I'm making so much money I've got to sit around every day just trying to figure what to do with it. That's why I'm here at this mine owners' meetin'. I even had to hire me a full-time lawyer to help me keep track of it. Tell Tap that Wade Eagleman's back in Denver, and he and Miss Rena are doin' well."

"Wade's your lawyer?"

"Yes, ma'am."

"Did you spend any of your money yet?"

"Angelita!" Pepper scolded.

"It's okay, Miss Pepper. Actually I did buy my sisters new houses."

"How many sisters do you have?" Angelita asked.

"Well, six of 'em are still alive."

"You bought six houses?"

"And a hotel."

"What hotel?"

"This one."

"You own the Alexandria?"

"Yes, ma'am. Ain't that somethin'?"

Pepper looked at the kind eyes of the tall, strong man who had spent years looking after her and the other girls at April's. "Stack, I can't think of anyone who deserves a break more than you."

"I can." Stack's shoulders slumped as he looked down at the white starched linen tablecloth.

"Who?"

"Rocky. You know, Miss Pepper, I took a wagon out to the Triple C and dug her up two weeks ago. I had her reburied on the side of Pingree Hill and put a big black stone marker on her grave."

Pepper brushed back the sudden tears.

He never stops looking after them, does he, Lord? Even when they're dead and buried, he keeps on taking care of them.

"Stack, you have just warmed my heart. This is the greatest news I've heard since little Tap, Jr., showed up down here." She patted her stomach.

"Tap, Jr.? Is that what you're goin' to name him?"

"Not really. But that's what Tap likes to call him."

"Or her," Angelita interjected.

"Miss Pepper, I can't tell you how glad I was to walk into this room and see you sittin' here. You girls was always family to me. Then you and Tap . . . well, I never took a likin' to any man faster than that husband of yours."

"Neither did I." Pepper grinned.

"And I was just plannin' on headin' up to Pine Bluffs and look you two up as soon as this meetin' is over."

"Oh, please do come by and spend a few days. Tap will love to talk to you, I'm sure."

"Yes, Miss Pepper, I think I will. I've got a business deal I'd like to talk to him about."

"What's that?"

"Now I ain't sure he'd be interested. But I got a chance to buy this ranch up in Montana Territory on the Yellowstone River. It's a 50,000-acre spread with good water and grass, but I don't know two squats about running cows. So here's what I was thinkin'. If I put up the money, maybe Tap could put up the work, and we'll halve the profits. You think he might go for that? I don't want to be interferin' with your family plans, but I'd sure like him to ponder it."

Pepper sat staring at Stack Lowery.

"Did I hear this conversation right? Did you just offer Tap half interest in a big Montana cattle ranch?"

"Yes, ma'am, I did. And I mean it. You think he might consider it?"

6

Although well dressed, Colton Banner leaned over his plate scraping down big hunks of meat and gravy like a man who lived all winter off tree bark and old boots. He wiped his hand across his mouth and then on his napkin.

"You lookin' for work?" Banner mumbled.

"I have more jobs than I can handle right now. Besides, I don't rustle cows."

Colton Banner's head came up with a wild look in his eyes. His fork dropped to his plate, and his right hand shot inside his coat, but the sound of Tap's .44 being cocked under the table brought his hand back in sight — empty.

"Are you callin' me a cattle thief?" Banner demanded.

"Aren't you?"

"Now, now, gentlemen," Selena cautioned. "It's supper time. I didn't come in here for you two to discuss business. I invited you to dine with us, Mr. Andrews, not shoot us. So if you'd slip that pistol back in the holster, we'll all try to be more pleasant. Now just what kind of jobs have been keeping a married gunslinger busy?" Selena's calm reflected her years of working in the constant confrontations of a dance hall.

"I'm a brand inspector out of Pine Bluffs."

"It was you?" Again Banner's hand went for his vest.

"Don't be silly, dear. Tapadera would shoot you down in a flash." Selena reached over and kept Banner's hand from reaching inside his coat. He forced her hand back with a loud slap. She grimaced but turned to Tap and tried to smile. "Now, Mr. Andrews, would you like to order some supper?"

Most of the people in the room now stared at their table.

"Think I'll eat somewhere else." Tap scooted his chair back. "You're choosing mighty poor company, Selena. Three of Banner's men jumped me last week."

"Yes, but you shot each of them dead, I heard. I'd say everything is all squared away. I'd like for you to stay. We'll just talk about old times."

Tap glanced over at Selena's flashing, almost pleading, brown eyes. *I'm not sure what she's sayin', Lord. Does she need me to help her?*

"Besides, if you go now, you'll never hear what's really happening to the cattle down along the South Platte," she argued.

"What's going on down there?"

"See? I knew you would be interested. Tell him, Colton."

"I ain't tellin' him nothin'."

"Well, then I'll tell him. How many cows were those three cowboys pushin' north?"

"Sixty-four."

"Last drive up from Texas, how many extras did your bosses end up with?"

"You mean, how many strays did they gather?"

"Strays? Well, I suppose that's what you call them. How many were in the gather?"

"About a hundred, I suppose."

"Then trying to recover sixty-four of a hundred isn't too greedy, is it."

"Are you telling me Tom Slaughter's crews stole your cattle?"

"What I'm sayin' is that they aren't particular where the bovines came from, just so they end up with more than they had when they began. But what if some small ranchers on the South Platte always seem to end up with cattle missing?"

"These were all TS beef before they had been rebranded."

"You're wastin' your time talkin' to the likes of him," Banner gruffed.

"Of course they were TS. The strays were sold off when they hit the tracks at Pine Bluffs. They're probably all hangin' in a Chicago meat packin' plant."

"You sayin' rustlin' is justified?"

"I'm sayin' some folks don't see it as rustlin' at all."

"Over the last fifteen years, 100,000 head have come up that trail. Many a head was lost to storms, stampedes, and Indians. Some of 'em brushed up and kept right on producin'. Those extras were unbranded mavericks."

Selena leaned her head lightly on her hands. "I can see we have an honest difference of opinion."

"Honest? There's nothin' honest about stealin' cattle, no matter how you try to justify it."

"We don't want you eatin' at our table!" Banner insisted.

Tap pushed back away from the table, shoved his Colt back into the holster, and walked toward the front door. Chairs scooted behind him. He heard Selena caution, "Don't be a fool, Colton!"

"Shut up!" Banner snarled.

He won't shoot me in the back, darlin'. Not in a crowded cafe. Not even ol' Colton Banner is that stupid. But I don't aim to give him a chance anywhere else.

"Andrews!"

It wasn't Colton Banner shouting.

"Wait up!"

Jacob Tracker dashed up to him at the hitching rail. "You leavin' already, Andrews? Shoot, we haven't even had a chance to eat supper."

"You're on your own in there. I signed on to bring you through the countryside, but I don't need to watch you at supper."

"No, but you want to eat, don't you?"

"I'll cook my own grub tonight."

"Who was the man with the lady?"

"Colton Banner."

"And just who is he?"

"He's the one who pays wages to that gang in Horse Creek Canyon."

"You mean, he's in charge of the rustlin'?"

"That's what I hear."

"Well . . . well, perhaps you should arrest him or something."

"I'm not a lawman, Tracker. Besides, I haven't caught him with any stolen bovines. It's just hearsay."

"Cabe and I will go ahead and finish supper. Where will you be campin'?"

Andrews pointed to the north. "Up by that butte."

"We'll be up in a couple hours," Tracker reported.

"Keep an eye on your poke. Not everyone in that room will treat you square."

Tap glanced back twice as he rode away from the stone barn at Running Water. Even in the twilight, no one was following him.

Camp turned out to be a low fire in a narrow trench — to hide the flames. Tap's back was against a boulder, with Roundhouse, still saddled, picketed not more than ten feet away.

Tap swirled his coffee in the tin cup and ripped another bite of pepper-spiced jerky off the long, narrow piece he held in his right hand. Long purple shadows stretched to the east as the stars began their twinkling appearance. The air felt tired and smelled like dead grass. A campfire or two glowed down closer to Running Water. His rifle lay beside him on top of his saddlebags.

Lord, I never know what to do with men like Banner. They don't draw on me; they hire someone else to do it. I'll never catch him stealin' cattle — or anything else. Yet if he weren't around, the others would wander off. He's the type that worries more about losin' the sixty-four beef than he does about losin' the men.

Tap pulled his revolver from the holster. With his blue tin cup in his left hand, he swigged a swallow of coffee, filtering the grounds with his teeth. He set the cup beside him and checked the cylinder of his gun, leaving the hammer set on the empty chamber, then replaced the gun in the holster, and picked up the cup again.

I'm too hotheaded, Lord. You know that. You knew that before You saved me. I reckon You were hopin' I'd change. But I don't know if I can now. I don't back down. I don't take bluff. I won't have someone threatenin' me.

He thought of Selena and Banner sitting at the table.

I wanted him to go for his gun. I wanted an excuse to shoot him. I never even thought about her. Lord, protect Selena. I don't know if she knows what she's got ahold of. She needs a good break or two, but this surely can't be somethin' You provided . . . can it?

It was hot by sunup and blazing by noon. Andrews rode ahead of the buckboard as they rambled down Old Woman Creek. They camped before sundown on the Leau Qui Court River. Tracker and Cabe spent most of the rest of daylight hiking to the top of the nearest butte to survey grazing lands on both sides of the river. The area resembled everything they had ridden through since they left Pine Bluffs — rolling

151

prairie, thick, short dried grass, scattered rock outcroppings, no trees except along the rivers or on the north sides of the few scattered mountains. Tracker and Cabe huddled by the fire and whispered plans late into the night. Tap easily ignored them.

The next morning they crossed the river, which ran no more than two feet deep. For two days they followed Black Thunder Creek and then the east fork of Lodge Pole Creek to some low rolling hills to the north.

Jacob Tracker pulled the buckboard to the base of one of the gradually sloping hills and parked it. He surveyed the landscape, turning in a full circle as he stood in the back of the wagon.

"This is it. This is the grazin' ground I've been lookin' for."

"You think there's enough water up here?"

"The creek runs in August, so I'm predictin' it still has water in November."

"It might be a wetter year than normal."

"Well, this is the main year I'm worried about," Tracker stated. "We'll need to mark it off."

"You makin' a claim?" Tap questioned.

"I certainly want some kind of legal description before I settle with the Land Office."

"You figure on payin' $1.50 an acre?"

"Perhaps less. I surmise there must be 30,000 to 40,000 acres in this drainage. What do you think?"

"I don't have the slightest idea," Tap admitted,

"but it will take you a few days to mark this out, won't it?"

"I reckon so."

"Then I gather my work is over. I brought you here. That was my part of the bargain."

"Yes, you did. But I do have one more chore," Tracker informed him.

Tap pulled on his bandanna and wiped his forehead. "What can I do for you?"

"I need you to ride to the nearest telegraph station and wire my trail boss with the location of this range."

"You haven't bought it yet."

"It will take months to get all the paperwork done. I expect to have cattle grazin' here within three weeks."

"What are you talkin' about?"

"I've got a herd comin' up the Goodnight-Lovin' Trail. They crossed the Colorado border two weeks before we rode on up to Pine Bluffs."

"How many head?"

"I've got 1,720."

"You're movin' 1,700 bovines and don't have a destination for them?"

Tracker swept his arm around the valley. "Oh, I have a destination now. Can you send the telegram?"

Tap rubbed his left leg but was unable to scratch the itch through chaps, duckings, boots, and socks. "Sundance Mountain will be the closest station."

"How long will that take you?"

"I'm guessin' it's fifty miles or so. Ridin' by myself, it will take me a good day to get there . . . if I don't get lost. I told you I don't know this country."

"You probably want to wait 'til mornin'."

"Yep. I don't aim on ridin' through unknown territory after dark."

"Let's make camp by those scrub cedars," Tracker suggested. "Might be a good place for a ranch house. What do you think, Andrews?"

Tap rode alongside the wagon. "I reckon so, but if I was living here, I'd put it right on that tableland at the bend of the creek. You can see most of the whole valley and still have a wind-break — the bluff to the west. You ought to be able to dig a well. If the underground channel is anything like the surface creek, then there ought to be a pool of water right back there. 'Course, you can do whatever you want when you buy the place. My opinion doesn't amount to much."

Tracker stopped the wagon, and Tap reined up.

"That's where you're wrong. I've been thinkin', Andrews. You interested in movin' up here and runnin' this part of the operation for me?"

"You want me to run a 30,000-acre spread?"

"Yep. I need to supervise things in Texas and on the trail. I need someone up here I can count on to hold it together when I'm gone. What do you think?"

"For salary or shares?"

"What do you want?"

"Both."

"We can discuss the terms later. I like shares. That way you have a direct interest in the operation, too."

"When are you goin' to need an answer?"

"Soon. I'll have the crew graze them until I get the paperwork settled."

"What about Cabe? How does he fit in?"

"He gets his shares, too, of course. But he doesn't have any interest in staying in this country any longer than he has to."

"You can say that again," Cabe bellyached. "I've already been out here a lot longer than I want."

"What do you think, Andrews?"

"We might work a deal. You swing by Pine Bluffs with the patent deeds, and we'll discuss it. I've got a wife that'll be deliverin' a baby in the fall. I'm not sure about the timin'."

Tap spent the evening sprawled on his bedroll, his foot propped on the saddle, his head on his saddlebags. The first stars blinked in a fading gray sky. He was still wide awake when the sky grew deep black. The stars swarmed like fireflies above his head.

Lord, it's next to perfect. A big spread far away from cities, saloons, gunfights. . . . Nothin' out here but fresh air and big blue skies.

And the wind.

I know, most days it's windy. But we can live with that. We'll need to build a ranch house, barn, bunkhouse, a shop, and some corrals. With half a dozen men, we can do that before winter. Angelita can help Pepper with the baby.

'Course, there's no school for Angelita. We'll just have to buy her a box of books. She reads well. Pepper and I can teach her all we know. That'll take about three days.

After a few years, my share will be a nice little herd. Then we can get our own place . . . closer to a town if Pepper wants. Wish Wiley was still up in the north country; he's a good hand. There's always plenty of men lookin' for work in Cheyenne in the spring; we can keep half a dozen during the winter.

We'll need to freight a few wagons of supplies over here before winter. If Stack's still runnin' out of Deadwood, he can bring us some goods. Haven't seen Lowery since May. Wouldn't mind havin' that big ol' piano man winter out with us. Couldn't offer him much, and he's got a good-payin' job.

We'll have to bring sawed lumber in for the buildings. There's just not enough timber around for log buildings. I could check out Sundance for supplies. I've got to find the quickest way to get there. This could be mighty lonely in the winters, I reckon.

"Andrews, you asleep yet?" Tracker called out from the fire.

"Nope."

"Been thinkin' about that offer I made ya?"

"Yep."

Jacob Tracker stood up and walked toward where Tap was lying. By instinct Tap slipped his hand down the handle of his revolver.

"I scratched out a telegram." Tracker handed the stiff folded paper to Tap. "Just send it to the station at Bushnell, Nebraska."

"Bushnell? You mean, you aren't drivin' them up through Pine Bluffs?"

"I told them to swing east. Too many herds around Pine Bluffs. I didn't want them gettin' mixed up with the others. 'Course, with your brand inspectin' I don't suppose I'd have had much trouble."

Tap sat up and gently massaged his bruised left leg. "This rascal is startin' to itch. Been thinkin' about ridin' to town tomorrow without a boot so I can scratch it. You want me to wait in Sundance for a reply?"

"Nope. I'm not sure when the herd will get there. Head on home when you're done."

"I'll probably drift back down on the Deadwood-Cheyenne road. You better do the same," Tap suggested. "We left those boys at Shaver's Crossing pretty steamed."

"You were the one that got them stirred up," Cabe reminded.

"Stirred 'em up? I saved your life."

"I don't need anyone to —"

Tracker boomed over Cabe's protest, "When we get through here, we'll come down the trail behind you. After I file for this land, I'll stop by your place and talk to you and the missus about movin' up here. You're goin' to be around Pine Bluffs for a while, aren't you?"

Tap noticed that his hand was still on the

walnut grip of his revolver. "I probably can work that out. I'll muster out before daylight. I want to make Sundance as soon as I can. So I won't be sayin' any howdys in the mornin'."

"I'll give you your pay tonight."

"It hasn't been a full two weeks."

"Don't matter. You earned it three times over." Tracker pulled out a leather bag from his vest pocket and counted out five twenty-dollar gold pieces.

"You're carrying a lot of coin," Tap mentioned.

"Don't trust them greenbacks. . . . Don't trust banks neither."

Just how much money does Tracker carry with him?

Tap crammed the coins into his britches pocket and laid back on his bedroll. "If I were you, I wouldn't trust Wes Cabe either."

"I've got a score to settle with you," Cabe hollered.

"Yeah . . . you and Ned Buntline ought go into writin' dime novels together," Andrews replied.

Sometime later Cabe and Tracker got into a heated argument that ended when both men grabbed the grips of their revolvers.

Lord, the deal of my life is opening up in front of me. This is the break I've been praying about. This could be our ranch!

Why is it I feel suspicious?

If Cabe's a partner in this ranchin' operation, You can deal me out. But if he's back in Texas . . . I

*could give it four or five good years and have my
own herd.*

Just before dark the next day Tap and Roundhouse cantered into the dusty settlement of Sundance Mountain. Tap's left foot was bare, and
his boot hung over the saddle horn. He swung
down off the saddle on the right side and handed
the reins to the dark-skinned livery operator with
big Spanish rowels on his spurs.

"What happened to your leg?" the man asked.

"Horse kicked it."

"That's the ugliest-lookin' foot I've ever seen
in my life."

"Thanks."

"You just stayin' in town one night?"

"Yep."

"That'll be four bits. In advance."

Tap dug some coins out of his vest pocket.
"Groom him from the offside, partner. He kicks
over there," Tap instructed.

"An Indian pony?"

"Maybe. I bought him from the IXL down in
Cheyenne."

"That blue roan in the third stall belongs to
an ol' boy who used to work the IXL. Meanest
horse I ever groomed."

Tap grabbed his rifle and tossed his saddlebags
over his shoulder as he headed for the barn door.
"Is he lookin' for a punchin' job?"

"The IXL man?"

"Yeah."

"Couldn't say. He's stayin' over at Pinky's." The man began to lead a reluctant Roundhouse inside the barn.

"What's his name? Maybe I'll look him up."

The man stopped and glanced back at Tap. "You hirin' cowhands?"

"There's a real good chance of it."

"He's new in town. I think he's called Odessa."

"Lorenzo Odessa?"

"Don't reckon I ever heard his first name."

"Does he carry a hogleg with a twelve-inch barrel strapped almost down to his knee?"

"That's him." The graying man smiled. "You know him?"

"Yeah . . . I know him."

Tap fought back the urge to go straight to Pinky's. Instead he hurried to the telegraph office, sent Tracker's message, and then, with Winchester still in hand, hiked back down the dusty dirt street toward an unpainted two-story, wood-frame building with a faded pink elephant painted on the false front.

The upstairs windows were all flung open, and white chintz curtains fluttered in the breeze. A dozen horses lined the front. A full-bellied man wearing worn coveralls was sound asleep on his back on the boardwalk.

Pinky's was part cafe, part dance hall, part billiard parlor, part hotel, but mostly a saloon. The ten-foot-tall, narrow front doors were propped open with rocks. Smoke and conversation rolled out into the street. Tap stepped into

160

the fifty-by-fifty-foot room. Once inside the door, he stood with his back to the near wall.

Must be some fellas figurin' on a quick exit — the back door has a card game perched next to it. . . . Three barmen . . . a couple serving girls . . . and a few workin' gals. And at the Faro table — Mr. Lorenzo Odessa himself.

Odessa's sandy-blond hair almost stuck straight out under his wide-brimmed dirty gray hat. Tap slipped around the side wall of the building. Carrying the Winchester in his left hand, he wove through the patrons until he hovered only a couple of feet behind Odessa.

Tap brought the barrel of the rifle up and let it rest on the nape of Odessa's neck.

"Kiss your Mary goodbye, Odessa, 'cause you're cashin' in more than your chips this time."

Odessa's hand flew for the rosewood grip of his highly modified .45. But a shove of the rifle barrel on the back of his neck made the wide-shouldered man hesitate to draw the weapon. He didn't turn around.

"Tapadera Andrews — the disgrace of Arizona! I rejoiced on the day I heard you were dead!"

"And I look forward to dancing on your grave, Lorenzo. By the looks of things, I won't have much longer to wait."

The Faro dealer stepped back from his layout. So did a dozen of Pinky's customers.

"I regret savin' your life when you were pinned under that dead pinto in the middle of Gila!" Odessa hissed.

"Me? It was you that was pinned under the horse when that redhead's daddy chased you out of his hacienda."

"That was me?"

"Yeah. And I was the one that had to duck buckshot and wade through hip-deep water."

"But who was it that rode his cayuse into the Golden Duck, then got bucked off into the roulette table, and had to be pulled out before a mob of screamin' miners sliced him into little strips?"

"That was me."

"Then I should never have pulled you out!" Odessa growled.

"You had to. You owed me."

Odessa stared out at the middle of the room. "For savin' me from drownin'?"

"No. You wanted me to introduce you to Junie Ann."

"Junie Ann . . . the Yellow Rose of Arizona? You introduced me to her?"

"You know I did." The rifle barrel still lay at Odessa's neck.

"She tried to kill me three times!"

"I regret her incompetence," Tap prodded.

A three-hundred-pound man wearing a bright pink shirt lunged out of the back room hoisting a double-barreled black-powder shotgun. "Would you two hurry up and kill each other so we can drag your bodies out and get that Faro game goin'!"

"Is that Pinky?" Tap asked.

"Yeah." Odessa winked at Tap and then said loudly for all to hear, "Boy, this is some low-class dive when a man can't greet an old pard without ever'one complainin'! Tapadera, you are a treat to look at, my friend. I heard you died in a prison cell in Yuma."

Tap lowered his rifle and slapped his arm around Odessa's shoulder. "And I heard a Sonoran señorita stuck you with a twelve-inch dagger."

"She broke my heart, Tap." Odessa grinned. "But she didn't stab me."

"If you two are through, I'd like to get my game goin'," the dealer interjected.

"Through!" Odessa shouted, pulling his huge revolver and pointing it at the dealer's now quivering head. "Through? When we get through, there won't be one man left alive in this building! I'll take twelve, and you take twelve, Tap."

"Who gets the big man with the old shotgun?"

"I'll take him; you get this Faro cheat." Odessa pointed the revolver at the man in the pink shirt while Tap jammed the rifle barrel into the dealer's belly.

The man's face turned snow-white.

Lorenzo Odessa broke into a deep, uncontrolled laugh.

"Forget it." Tap grinned at those at the bar. "We were only jokin'. Relax. Odessa's buyin' ever'one a drink."

"I'm what?" Odessa wheezed.

Tap pointed to the flat rectangular chips.

"Those blue markers are your winnin's, aren't they?"

"But —"

"Come on, you tightwad!"

"But . . . but," Lorenzo protested, "you don't even drink!"

"Well, these men do. Right, boys?"

With a shout and a roar, everyone in the building except Tap and Odessa headed to the bar.

"It's good to see you, Tap. I really did think you were dead."

"Pay your tab. Then let's go out on the porch and talk," Tap suggested.

Tap was sitting on a flat bench behind the sleeping man when Lorenzo Odessa finally sauntered out, sporting worn batwing chaps and his spurs jingling.

"You cost me six dollars!" Odessa complained.

"That's what you get for leavin' your back to the door. You didn't used to be so careless."

"Shoot, nobody knows me up here."

"They do now."

The clean-shaven cowboy plopped down next to Tap on the worn wooden bench. "That old boy has been sleepin' there all day." He pointed to the big man in the coveralls. "With all that lipstick on his neck, I've been wonderin' just how good a time he had last night."

"What are you doin' here, Lorenzo? I thought you went back to west Texas for good."

"I came up the trail with the IXL herd in the spring and then hired on to work in Johnson

County. But it's goin' crazy over there. They're shootin' each other for grazin' rights."

"I don't remember you backin' down from many a fight," Tap observed.

"I ain't that young anymore. I just don't feel like dyin' for someone else's bovines. If they was mine, it might be different. How about you? Did you get run out of Arizona?"

"More or less. But that's all cleared up now. I'm workin' as brand inspector down around Pine Bluffs."

"Brand inspector?" Odessa roared. "Sounds like you've taken up the rockin' chair."

"With the amount of rustlin' goin' on, it's never boring. Besides, there's a lot of things different in my life now."

"Oh, sure." Lorenzo laughed. "Let me guess . . . Tap Andrews, gunfighter and every gal's favorite, took himself a wife, has three kids, and teaches Sunday school."

"You got it, partner."

Odessa spun around and stared at Tap. "I was only joshin'," he mumbled.

"I wasn't," Tap replied.

"You mean . . ."

"I've got a beautiful wife who's expectin' our first in a few months. We're raisin' a friend's ten-year-old daughter, and, no, I don't teach Sunday school, but you'll find me there most ever' week."

"Well, I'll be! . . . I never figured either of us would ever live this long, let alone settle down."

"Yeah." Tap leaned back against the side of the building. "I keep thankin' the Lord for my blessin's."

"Tapadera, that's truly inspirin'."

"Inspirin'?"

"I've been here a couple days just picking up some winnin's and ponderin' where I should go next. I keep thinkin' I should go home . . . and then I remember I got no home to go to."

"You lookin' for work?"

"You hirin'?"

"Maybe."

"You hirin' me to use my gun or my rope?" Odessa asked.

"Your rope. I think I'm goin' to need a top hand to put together a ranchin' operation."

"You ain't goin' over to Johnson County, are you?"

"Nope. About fifty miles south of here on the top edge of Black Thunder Basin."

"What kind of operation?"

"This old boy from Texas is bringin' 1,700 head up to a 30,000-acre spread he's goin' to buy. It's a brand-new outfit in the middle of nowhere. He's asked me to foreman the place on shares. I'll have to have half a dozen men full time and the rest hired as needed."

"You reckon I could buy in and start buildin' a little herd for myself?" Odessa asked.

"Yep."

Odessa pushed his hat back, uncovering his curly blond hair and blue eyes. "I'm your man, partner!" He reached out and shook Tap's callused hand. "Who is this Texas man?"

"Goes by the name of Jacob Tracker."

"Tracker. Jake Tracker? That no-good backshootin' son of a . . . buffalo chip!"

"Whoa, what do you know about Tracker? Is this the same man?"

"Is he in his early fifties, dark hair with gray streaks, about five-foot-ten, narrow dark eyes, and kind of bushy sideburns?"

"Sounds like him. What's the deal about Tracker, Odessa?"

"The Tobbler place was burned out on the Pecos. The whole family and hired hands were shot. Ever'one blamed the Mexicans. In fact, the troops crossed the border into Sonora lookin' for the culprits, but no trace was found.

"The family that was left, two sisters in San Angelo, hired some of us boys to go and round up the Tobbler stock and kind of settle accounts. We only brushed out 600 head."

"How many were they supposed to have?"

"The bank had made a loan on 2,100 head."

"So there were 1,500 missing?"

"Yep . . . maybe more because the loan was before calvin' started."

"What does Tracker have to do with this?"

"Rumor has it that he was run out of New Mexico by old John Chisum personally. Tracker gathered a gang of hangers-on and gamblers — not exactly cowhands, but he knew cattle. And about three weeks after the Tobbler massacre,

Tracker showed up outside Amarillo pushin' a big herd of Lazy T beef."

"Tobbler's?"

"Yep. But he had a bill of sale and said he paid cash for the herd. Now no one had any idea where he got the cash to buy them. But no one could prove that he didn't, so while the lawyers debated the law, Tracker pushed them out of state, paid off the gunslingin' crew that proceeded to roar their way across Texas . . . and that ended the matter."

"Is that the gospel truth, Lorenzo?"

"I buried some of the Tobblers myself, Tap. It's the gospel truth."

"How in the world did a character like that get enough money to buy a big ranch?"

"Maybe he ain't buyin' it," Lorenzo suggested.

"But he wanted me to run the place and —"

"To hold 'em over the winter while he peddled them off in the Black Hills. You do the work, take the risks. He ain't drover enough to hold them over the winter."

Tap stood up and paced the boardwalk. His spurs and jinglebobs sang tenor while his boot heels thundered the bass.

"I can't believe he hooked me like that! I can't believe it! I bailed that man out three or four times," Tap fumed.

A voice boomed from the porch, "You goin' to stomp around like that all day? I might as well git up and eat my breakfast."

Tap and Lorenzo looked over at the big man

168

in coveralls as he groaned, sat up, and rubbed the stubble of a two-week beard. Struggling to his feet, he staggered toward the front door of Pinky's.

"Do you know a man named Cabe — Wesley Cabe?"

"Is he runnin' with Tracker?"

"They were together."

"I wouldn't turn my back on that Cabe. Some say he was the one that shot them two girls at Big Sarah's in the back."

"I can't believe this, Lorenzo! I just spent a week baby-sittin' those two."

"Did you get your pay?"

"Yep."

"And you didn't take any lead? I'd say you got by just fine."

Andrews plopped back on the bench next to Odessa and stretched out his legs.

"You limpin', Tap?"

"Oh, I got a horse that busted up my leg. It's gettin' better."

"I got myself a mean horse, too. I'd trade him in a minute, but nobody would take him."

Tap stared out into the street.

Lord, I don't know how I could have been suckered along like that. Used to be I didn't trust anyone. Figured ever'one was out to cheat me. But lately I cut 'em a break . . . believe their line and get taken in. I've got to quit this business before I get shot in the back.

"Odessa, you got a few days you can spare me?"

169

"I ain't holdin' down wages if that's what you mean."

"How about ridin' down to the Black Thunder Basin and facin' down this Tracker with me? I don't much care for gettin' sucked in like that."

"It beats stayin' around here buyin' drinks for the house."

"Is there a decent meal served in this town?"

"Nope."

"Is there one that a man with a strong stomach can keep down?" Tap probed.

"Louisa's will stick with you."

"I'm going to grab some supper. I'll meet you at daybreak at the livery, and we'll ride south."

Evening shadows began to fall on Sundance. Lorenzo Odessa reached out and poked Andrews. "The country's different, but you and me ridin' out together . . . sort of feels like the old days in Tucson, don't it?"

"Only this time no one's chasin' us, and we didn't get run out of town."

"At least, not yet!" Odessa whooped.

With daylight just breaking in the east, Tap could barely see his way down Sundance's one street as he hobbled to the livery to retrieve Roundhouse. His left knee was stiff, and he limped along, toting his saddlebags over his right shoulder and cradling his Winchester in his left arm.

He had the big gray saddled and ready to ride by the time Odessa showed up. The liveryman insisted that Lorenzo saddle his own horse.

"Tap," Lorenzo hollered as he walked the horse out in front of the corrals, "you better give me some room. This old boy still has some kinks in him."

Andrews mounted Roundhouse from the off side and then spun him three times to the right, then three times to the left. The gray horse settled right down, so Tap rode him over next to the corral gate and waited.

"Okay, Odessa, let's see your show."

The muscular cowboy jammed his left foot in the stirrup and swung up into the Texas saddle. He had not found his seat when the horse began to buck wildly.

After the blue roan's first jump, Odessa grabbed the saddle horn, and Roundhouse got inspired to join in. The jolt of the first unexpected leap caused Tap to drop the reins. Because he couldn't turn the horse, Roundhouse plunged and bucked straight ahead — toward Lorenzo and his horse.

It was on Roundhouse's fourth jump, with Tap clutching the horn and the retrieved reins, that the horse made a sudden lunge almost straight left. Tap didn't even see it coming, but Odessa's horse jumped right at that moment. The two horses met in an explosive head-on crash.

The blow tossed Tap to the left side of the saddle, jamming his left foot in the stirrup and causing a searing pain to shoot up his leg. Round-house staggered backwards shaking his head.

Lorenzo Odessa's horse went down and in fright started kicking wildly. But Odessa's leg was pinned under the horse, and he couldn't yank it free. He could only try to duck the flying hooves.

"Shoot the horse!" Odessa shouted.

Tap reached for his rifle in the scabbard, but the sudden movement caused Roundhouse to bolt straight down the main street of town at a gallop. Unable to stop the horse, Tap sprinted him around to the north and circled him behind the buildings, racing him back to the corrals. By the time he arrived, Odessa's horse was up and circling back toward the barn. Lorenzo was brushing layers of dirt off his shirt, his britches, his hat, and his sandy-blond hair.

The liveryman sat on the top rail of the corral and roared. "Them rich people down there in Cheyenne City will pay good money to see you boys put on a show like that!"

"Why didn't you shoot him?" Odessa yelled out.

"My horse was buckin', too. I surmised that I might shoot you by mistake."

"Either way would've worked. Now would you get that horse of yours out of here so I can get mounted?"

Tap rode Roundhouse down the street about fifty yards from the corral. He watched at a distance as Odessa climbed back into the saddle. This time the blue roan tore off on a gallop in the opposite direction.

That's the wrong way, Lorenzo. You'll be in

Deadwood before I can get you spun around.

They detoured him within a quarter of a mile. Then Tap and Lorenzo rode south across the rolling prairie and into another hot, breezeless day.

Near sunset they reached the pass just above the top of Black Thunder Basin. Tap rode straight for the tiny clump of cedars.

"I didn't figure they'd ride on yet. I pictured them sittin' right here and waitin' for the herd to arrive."

"Maybe they're camping on down the creek somewhere," Lorenzo guessed.

"That could be."

"Shoot!" Tap shouted. "The whole reason for this charade was to get the brand inspector out of the country when they moved that herd through from Texas! Send me north. Then send me back on the Deadwood/Cheyenne road and have me wait at Pine Bluffs. They got me clear out of the picture without havin' to shoot me. I can't believe I could be so gullible."

Odessa rode his horse in between the scrub cedars.

"The whole thing is just a plot by Tracker to get me away from the stolen cattle. He ain't buyin' anything but just parkin' 'em up here and peddlin' them off. He wasn't even plannin' on me runnin' the spread," Tap hollered in disgust.

"Well, something must have gone wrong with

the plan," Odessa shouted back.

"Why's that?"

"Because," Odessa pointed to the ground behind the cedar trees, "Jake Tracker is laying over here stone-dead."

7

"Looks like he got a couple of bullets in the back," Odessa shouted.

Andrews slipped off Roundhouse and led the horse to the cedars. The soft red dirt dusted his black boots as he dug in his heels and climbed the knoll. He handed the reins up to Odessa and squatted to examine Tracker's body.

"The blood's dried and cracked . . . the body's stiff." Tap rolled him over and shut his eyelids. "He's been dead awhile. His poke's gone, but his gun's still in the holster. Don't know many bushwhackers who wouldn't lift a man's pistol."

"It sure wasn't Indians," Odessa added.

"Nope. Wind has blown most of the tracks away. You don't see another body, do you?"

"Cabe?"

"Yeah. Circle around and see if you can spot anything. Maybe somebody jumped 'em. The Platte River Boys at Shaver's Crossin' were gun-slingin' mad when we left 'em. Maybe they trailed us up here after all."

Tap pushed his hat back and inspected the ground. "If Cabe's not dead, then he's a prime suspect. I don't see any wagon around either."

After a quick, futile search, both men returned to the cedars.

"What I know of Wes Cabe," Odessa offered, "he'd sure enough shoot someone in the back

175

just to lift a poke. But I'd have thought they'd try to plant you back down in one of these little canyons."

"No need to shoot the brand inspector if you can sucker him into bein' on your side."

"But if the two of them were in cahoots, why shoot it out? They hadn't got to the big money yet," Odessa pondered.

"Maybe Cabe didn't like his percentage. Anyway, he has some explainin' to do. If he's alive, I can't figure any good reason he left Tracker lyin' here."

"Tap, what are we going to do with this old boy?"

"Bury him in a shallow grave, I reckon."

With dirty cotton sleeves rolled up, Andrews and Odessa scooped out some of the soft dirt in the midst of the cedars with the butts of their rifles and rolled Tracker into it. While Odessa covered the body, Tap hefted a few boulders to mark the spot.

Lord, have mercy on his soul. I'm buryin' men I don't even know. I was mad enough to shoot him myself last night . . . but seein' him lyin' here . . . well, there's more to life than stolen cattle, makin' money, and firin' a .45 at a man's back. I don't aim to end my life layin' dead in the cedars.

Andrews and Odessa made camp at the bend in the creek. It was a clear, warm night, but toward morning a few clouds streaked overhead. Tap smelled sulphur in the air. By daylight it was clear again, but the air was humid and sticky.

It's a shallow-breathin', slow-movin' day. If we were home, I'd go down to the ice house and see if there were any chunks left hidin' in the straw.

Roundhouse made only a minimum protest at being mounted. Odessa's horse turned around and bit at Lorenzo's ear but only managed to take a small chunk out of his hat. In response Odessa cracked a two-inch piece of firewood across the horse's nose. To both men's relief, the blue roan caught a temporary case of good manners and stood perfectly still.

After a couple of circles around the grove of squat cedars, Tap and Odessa picked up the buckboard tracks leading southeast down Black Thunder Creek. For most of the way, they followed the exact route the buckboard had taken two days earlier.

"Where's Cabe goin'?" Odessa asked.

"Looks like he's headed back to Running Water."

"Don't make sense, does it? If he and Tracker got into a scrap over them rustled cattle, why not wait here and assume control of the herd?"

Tap and Odessa kept their horses at a fast walk side by side as they rode down out of the basin. "Cabe wasn't a cattleman. He couldn't tell a heifer from a steer. Maybe he was satisfied with the poke. But that type usually is consumed with greed. Chances are he's cookin' up some plan to get more for himself."

"You think Tracker really was carryin' a lot of money?"

Tap sat straight up and broke Roundhouse into a trot by signaling the horse with his knees. "I reckon he had the funds to pay off the cowhands bringing up the herd."

"If Wes Cabe just wanted the poke, he could have shot Tracker in Colorado and saved time."

"Cabe didn't seem smart enough to do much more than cheat at three-card monte, but I've never been able to think like a man who shoots someone in the back. Maybe there's a few answers waitin' for us up the trail."

It was near sunset when they crested the pass and looked down on the stone barn at Running Water. Tap's bandanna slouched like a wet red rag about his neck. His shirt was soaked with sweat. His vest was rolled up and tied to his cantle. The dirt had turned to mud in the folds of his neck.

"There's a few wagons down there, Tap. You recognize any of them?"

Running Water looked more like a stage stop than a settlement. "Not yet." Tap spurred Roundhouse into the lead. He pulled his Winchester from the scabbard, checked the lever, and then laid it across his lap.

"How we goin' to play this, Tap?"

Andrews gazed over at the leathery, chiseled face of Lorenzo Odessa. "You remember how we used to do ever' time we went into a new little Mexican pueblo?"

"You mean, I come in five minutes behind you

and bail you out?" It was a deep laugh . . . one built on years of shared adventures.

"Bail me out? You'd always run off with some señorita, and I didn't see you for days!"

"That didn't happen more than . . . half a dozen times, did it?"

Ignoring Odessa, Andrews tugged his hat down tight on his head as they rode through a dust devil and then pushed it back up when the wind died down. "That far buckboard looks like Cabe's. He must not be expectin' company, since he's corralled the horses. That cafe has a back door. It's all supper tables except for a poker game right inside the back. You come through that way. I don't think Cabe will make a play unless he can shoot you in the back. Let's flush him outside and see what he has to say. We just might have to turn him in at Ft. Laramie."

"He might have friends in there."

"He sure acted like a stranger the first time we came through. But I've surely been wrong a lot lately," Andrews admitted. "Might be some folks in there that know me, but none of 'em know you, Odessa. I'll concentrate on Cabe. You watch for his friends."

"It's just like old times, Tapadera."

"It hasn't been that long ago, has it?"

"You got to be old to have old times. I keep tellin' you, we're old." Lorenzo laughed. "I'll back your play to my last bullet, partner."

Odessa swung off the trail to the west and circled around the corrals.

Lord, a man don't get too many friends like that. Old times? We're older, all right. Wiser, I suspect. Being foolhardy is a young man's game. I truly ask that we both live long enough to be really old, old friends.

Andrews trotted Roundhouse up the road. His back was straight. Face expressionless. Eyes focused. Winchester propped across his saddle. At a distance, it was hard to tell if his dark complexion revealed an inheritance from his mother or the results of six months in the sun or merely dirt.

That's Tracker's buckboard. Lord, there's somethin' that troubles me. If all Lorenzo said about Tracker is true, then I'm not sure that he didn't deserve what he got. Maybe this is all just Your justice, and I should let it drop.

He pulled up next to a crowded hitching rail.

Who am I kiddin'? I want him to make a play. They strung me along and got me away from my job, and I want to get even.

Lord, I've been thinkin' that way too long. I want justice — that's all! But You've got to help me remember that.

Tap tied Roundhouse to the right side of the hitching rail. He noticed two men standing at the far end of the cafe's front porch. They seemed content to gaze out into the darkening road. He stared for a moment at the backs of their heads.

You boys are waitin' for somethin'. But it can't be me, can it? You didn't know I was comin' this way. I didn't know I was comin' back this way.

180

Have I seen you before?

Tap fidgeted with his saddlebags, trying to get a clearer glimpse of their faces. He started to pull his rifle and then shoved it back into the scabbard.

Platte River Boys? They shaved up and changed clothes. Are they followin' me . . . or just a lucky coincidence? They didn't seem like the type to make a stand at a public cafe. Maybe the rest of 'em are inside. I'm just lookin' for Cabe, and I might have uncovered the whole rat's nest. Nothin's ever as simple as you plan.

Tap pulled five brass cartridges from his bullet belt and dropped them into the right pocket of his brown leather vest. There were two steps to the top of the boardwalk in front of the building, and both jolted his tender left knee. He felt his eyes squint at the burst of pain. The two men at the other end of the porch continued to stare in the opposite direction. Neither moved or said a word.

Okay, Lord, I'm walkin' into a trap. But they don't know that I know that I'm walkin' into a trap. That gives me the odds.

I think.

Tap hiked straight toward the front door of the cafe. He heard the boots and spurs of the two men easing in behind him. He spun on his heels, pulled his .44, and cocked it as he lifted it toward the head of the man on his right. His left hand gripped the wrist of the other man and kept him from drawing his pistol.

Both hesitated, hands resting on holstered revolvers.

"You boys aren't followin' me, are you?" Tap growled.

"Eh . . . no, sir," the younger of the two replied, his head only inches away from the barrel of Tap's cocked Colt.

"We was jist goin' to have us some supper," the other mumbled.

"Oh, that's good." Tap nodded and stepped back from the door. He released the man's wrist but didn't lower his gun. "Why don't you go in first? You boys are probably a lot hungrier than I am."

"No, sir, you go right ahead."

"You two are goin' ahead of me. If someone's goin' to get shot in the back, I don't aim on it bein' me." Tap smiled from ear to ear. "You know, I've been thinkin' . . . if I was to pull the trigger on this .44, would the bullet go clear through your skull and hit your buddy right behind the ear, or would I have to shoot him separate? What do you think?"

"I think we ain't hungry anymore."

"No, sir, we ain't. I reckon we'll just ride on out of here. Come on, Utah."

"You aren't goin' anywhere . . . yet." Tap laid the barrel of his pistol on the temple of the younger man. "What are you Platte River Boys doin' up here? I told you at Shaver's I'd shoot anyone who followed us."

"We ain't followin' you. Besides, we have a

right to eat anywhere we want. That is, if we was hungry, which we ain't."

"Since you lost your appetite, you just walk real slow out to the corrals. I don't want to shoot you right in front of the cafe. It might spoil someone's supper."

"You ain't goin' to shoot us!" one man cried out.

"You were ready to ambush me."

"Well, it ain't nothin' personal. We get fifty dollars each if we shoot you."

"Now who's goin' to pay you that?"

"Don't tell him nothin', Cotton!"

"You ain't got the gun aimed at your head, Utah."

"He won't shoot you."

"He shot Texas Jay."

"Who's goin' to pay you?"

"Banner. Colton Banner said he would give us fifty dollars each if we killed you."

"Cotton, shut your mouth!"

"Utah, ain't you goin' to do nothin' to help me?" the younger one pleaded.

"I ain't goin' to do nothin' to get your head shot off neither. Mister, we didn't pull a gun on you, and we didn't threaten your life. We told you the truth. Now we jist want to git on our horses and ride out of here. Ain't no crime in that, is there?"

"If you come at me again, I'll shoot you on sight. You know that, don't you?"

"Mister, there're easier ways to earn fifty dollars. You won't see us."

"Get out of here." Tap motioned with the .44.

"Yes, sir. Come on, Utah, let's lift some dust."

"He'll shoot us in the back with that Winchester."

"That's better than being shot in the head from only an inch away. Come on."

Tap walked the men to their horses, his gun still pointed at them. As they rode south, he walked behind the hitched horses and shuffled around to Roundhouse's right side.

If they swing back, I could be pinned in from both sides. And if they've got friends inside, it's going to get mighty dangerous. Maybe I ought to sneak around to the back and pull Odessa out of there.

Andrews had just loosed the big gray's lead rope and looped it on the horn when two gun blasts sent him diving to the dirt in the street. Roundhouse reared, and Tap rolled in the dirt to keep from being trampled. He yanked his gun and pointed it toward the front door, but he could see nothing. The front doors of the cafe remained closed.

Inside? They're shootin' inside! Lorenzo? What's he done? Maybe those two really were workin' on their own. The others don't even know I'm out here!

Grappling to his feet, Tap brushed the dirt off and glanced around to see if anyone was watching him. He quickly retied a jittery Roundhouse. His left leg almost gave out as he struggled up the steps. The front doors of the cafe swung open, and several men hustled out. All three went straight for their horses, ignoring Tap and leaving the front door open. With black hat pulled low and right hand on the walnut grip of his holstered .44, he slipped into the cafe.

Almost every gun in the room was pulled and pointed at the rear of the building where a man, holding a badly bleeding shoulder, sprawled across the worn green felt-covered table. Standing at the back door, Lorenzo Odessa faced the crowd with his hands in the air and his pistol in his holster. The bitter taste of black powder filtered through the tobacco smoke. Wes Cabe was not in the room, nor was Colton Banner or Selena.

Tap slipped his gun out of his Mexican loop holster and pointed it at Odessa just like the others.

"Good work, boys!" Tap shouted. "You caught that polecat Odessa! Ought to be a reward for someone."

An older man pointed to the wounded man. "Big Earl spotted him first."

"Good work, Earl." Tap nodded. "You better get a doc to look at that shoulder."

He moved through the crowd straight at Odessa. "You go for that gun, Lorenzo, and I'll gut-shoot you and let you die a painful death right on the floor of this cafe!"

"Andrews, you ain't ever stopped me before, and you cain't stop me now! Come on, let's go outside. I'll take you on one to one!"

"You aren't takin' on anyone, Odessa. You'll

swing from the lamppost at Pine Bluffs when they find out the biggest rustler in the territory is caught. Now where's that no-good partner of yours?"

"He's got a partner?" one of the men asked. Suddenly they were turning their guns on each other, scouting the crowd.

"A burnt-faced gambler with slick hands and a weak back. Wears a round brown hat and goes by the name of Wes Cabe. I've been followin' his buckboard. It's out there next to the corral. None of you happened to shoot him, did ya? There's a reward for him, too."

"I sold him a horse," one man shouted.

"How do you know so much about rewards?" another asked.

"Because brand inspectors are supposed to know those things."

"You claimin' to be a brand inspector?"

"Hey," a thin man at the back asked, "didn't you used to be a deputy in Cheyenne?"

"Yep."

"You the one that laid Del Gatto in the grave?"

"Yep."

I have no idea if they are Del Gatto's friends or enemies.

"Well, shoot," the man drawled, "I ain't goin' up against the man that leaded down old Alex Del Gatto."

Several in the room holstered their guns. Some sat back down to supper.

"You say there is a reward for this hombre?"

someone shouted.

"I guarantee that every penny I make off him I'll send to Big Earl."

"Go on, take your prisoner, brand inspector," another man called out. "Besides, Big Earl drew first. He ain't exactly the smartest man in Wyomin'." Muted laughter sprang up around the room.

"What happened to Cabe?" Andrews asked.

"He rode off with Banner."

Cabe partnered up with Colton Banner? And I just sent Banner's boys down the trail to warn them! That was real smart, Andrews.

"What about Miss Selena? Was she with them?"

"That purdy black-haired girl?"

"Yeah, what about her?" Tap demanded.

"I reckon she went with 'em. She's been sick in her room for a couple of days. Ain't none of us seen her."

"They travel in a carriage?" Tap asked.

"No, sir, they all bought horses. My best bay mare, in fact. And two fast black geldings."

"When did they leave?"

"Last night. You goin' after them?"

"Depends on when I decide to shoot Odessa."

"You goin' to kill him?" one grizzled prospector with bright red hair asked.

"Not until he tries to escape. That reward is only good if he's alive to testify in court."

A big man with a long beard and rope suspenders boomed out, "I ain't trustin' him. Think

I'll just ride back to Pine Bluffs with 'em and collect that reward money myself."

"Partner, that's fine with me. Since you're taggin' along, how about you leadin' Odessa's blue roan around to the rail in front where my pony is hitched. He's tied up in back, but don't try to ride that horse. He's too hot-blooded."

"Horse ain't been made I couldn't ride," the man blustered. His greasy britches were tucked into new stove-top black boots.

"Maybe so, but whatever you do, don't mount that horse!" Tap insisted as he began shoving Odessa toward the front door.

"I'll kill you, Andrews!" Odessa shouted. "So help me, I'll tie you to a wagon wheel and burn your skin off just like those Apaches!"

"Odessa, I surely wish you'd just make a break for it so I could shoot you right now and save the county some money!"

Everyone in the room followed Tap and Lorenzo out the door to the porch. Most had their guns jammed back into their holsters. The bearded man meandered around the corner of the building leading the blue roan, who plodded along, head down, ears tucked back.

"I thought you said you could ride that horse, Owen!" someone shouted from the crowded porch.

"If a man tells me not to ride his horse, I don't ride it. That's the code," he explained.

"Ride the outlaw and get your head busted up. I don't give a hoot," Odessa challenged.

"Don't do it, Owen," Tap protested. "He's just tryin' to get you hurt."

"He gave you permission," someone shouted. "I heard him! I heard him!"

Owen grabbed the latigo with both hands and tightened the cinch. Then he looped the reins in his large, callused left hand as he grabbed the horn and jammed his left boot into the stirrup. Just as his full weight settled into the oxbow and he began to throw his right leg across the saddle, the blue roan broke loose, twisting to the right and kicking his hind legs skyward. On the third frantic buck, Owen catapulted right over the horse's head and landed in the dirt on his right shoulder. The horse continued to buck and twist, spinning 180 degrees. Owen tried to sit up and caught the full force of both hind hooves right under his back shoulder blades. He flew through the air about twelve feet across the street, jumped up with nothing but the whites of his eyes peering out of his head, then fell unconscious, face first, into the street.

"I tried to tell him!" Tap shouted. "I guess this means Owen won't be travelin' with us. Keep Odessa covered."

Andrews led Roundhouse out to the middle of the street and mounted from the right side. The horse stood and waited for a signal.

That-a-boy. One bad horse is enough. Just stay calm, big boy.

The blue roan stopped bucking and stood deceptively calm in the middle of the street. Tap rode Roundhouse over behind him and pulled out his rifle. Flipping up the upper tang long-range peep sight, he motioned to the others with guns still drawn. "Let Odessa mount up."

"What if he makes a run for it?" someone shouted.

"Then I get to shoot him!"

Odessa sauntered by Tap. "I kin hardly wait to put a knife in yer back, Andrews!"

"Just don't get bucked off," Tap grumbled in deep tones with his teeth clenched.

The blue roan didn't buck a bit when Lorenzo Odessa mounted, but he did take off on a gallop south. Roundhouse immediately bolted right behind him. Tap clamped his knees tight and raced after Odessa.

They didn't slow down until the buildings at Running Water sank out of sight on the northern horizon. Tap led them off the road to the east. They finally stopped on top of a ridge and looked back at the road.

"Anyone followin' us?" Odessa asked, wiping the sweat off his face with his bandanna.

Tap took a deep breath and let out a sigh. "Nope."

"I can't believe we've been together only one day and already had to make a break out of town."

Tap shrugged. "Running Water's not what I call a town. But I did have to bail you out. What in the world happened in there?"

"I just slipped in the back door like you said.

I leaned up against the wall and watched the poker game, waitin' for you to come in. Well, this greasy-headed hombre with the Montana crease hat . . . the one they called Big Earl . . . looks up after losin' a substantial pot. He spies me and yells, 'You!' Then he jumps to his feet and goes for his gun. Naturally, I decided it would be to my advantage to shoot first. So I did."

"Who was he?"

"I don't have any idea. We've been around too long, Tap. I don't even remember 'em anymore. When I walk into a room, I can't tell if it's filled with friends or enemies. I didn't reckon anyone knew me up here. I guess he didn't like my looks."

"That's understandable."

Odessa turned his horse and trotted alongside Andrews as they headed east. "What took you so long, Andrews? Seems like I was camped in there with a room full of guns pointin' at me for a long time."

"I ran into a couple of the Platte River Boys standin' on the porch. They said Banner had a fifty-dollar bounty on my head."

"No foolin'?" Odessa pushed back his hat and grinned a mouthful of straight white teeth. "Fifty ain't much, but it would buy me a new saddle and some tobacco."

"You aren't goin' to collect it!" Tap frowned. "What happened to those two on the porch?"

"I ran 'em off."

"Without firin' a shot?"

"Not ever'one has to shoot their way out of a fix."

"He drew on me, Tap. What choice did I have?" Odessa griped. "So they hightailed it back to the North Platte to warn 'em all that you are on the trail."

"At the time, I didn't reckon Cabe had partnered up with 'em. Sounds a lot like two snakes sharin' the same hole. I didn't figure right."

"Yeah. I didn't calculate you'd sit out on the porch visitin'. I thought you'd bust through that door after you heard the shootin'. What were you waitin' for — a formal invitation?"

"I . . . eh, I was flat on the ground."

"Did they pin you down?"

"No. When I heard the shots, I surmised someone was throwin' lead at me. I couldn't figure why others weren't coming out the front door. By the time I realized what was goin' on, they had you nailed to the back wall. That's not exactly what I planned on us doin'."

"But you found out about Cabe."

"Yeah. Now we're trailin' him and all the sneak thieves and rustlers of Laramie County."

"Sort of feels like two years ago in Bisbee. Another place you and me better not visit again. Where are we headed, Tap? We goin' to take on that whole gang?"

"Cabe left with Banner, and Banner's runnin' that crew of horse thieves and rustlers at Platte Crossing and up Lone Tree Canyon. I'm guessin'

Cabe and Banner made some sort of deal with the Texas herd. So if you've got the time, maybe we could go to North Platte Crossing and nose around . . . to scout what's going on. Then up to Lone Tree and maybe swing out to Nebraska to find the Texas beef."

"I'll tell you what I want, Mr. Tapadera Andrews. I want to be part of the crew that pushes those cows back to the Tobblers in Texas."

"Sounds good to me. I just want to make sure Banner and Cabe get stopped."

"Who's this Miss Selena you kept askin' about?"

"She's a friend of Pepper's . . . well, not really a friend. She and Pepper used to work dance halls together."

"Is she 'pretty as a prairie on a spring day'?"

Tap looked over at Lorenzo and laughed. "You aren't still usin' that same old line, are you?"

"It don't ever fail, Tap."

"She's a pretty girl who's had a hard life and is runnin' with a rough crowd. If you ever get close enough . . . well, watch out for the sneak gun and the long-bladed knife."

Lorenzo grinned. "Sounds like my kind of woman!"

"We're goin' after rustlers and murderers — not señoritas. If we let them hide in a hole with a gang to back 'em up, we aren't goin' to flush 'em out too easy. The quicker we catch up with them, the fewer guns they'll have," Tap added.

"They've got a head start. You don't think

Cabe and Banner will just be sittin' around this Shaver's Crossin', do you?"

Tap slipped his rifle back into the leather scabbard. "I think Cabe and Banner will shoot each other in the back first chance they get."

"And you want to stop them from doin' that?"

"I want someone to pay for shootin' Tracker in the back. And I want to make sure those Texas beef get turned around."

"It don't have anything to do with a little vengeance and gettin' even for stringin' you along, does it?" Odessa grinned.

Tap's only answer was a glare.

After dark they set up a cold camp on Old Woman Creek. Within minutes the mosquitoes discovered them with vicious delight. Tap led a retreat to a knoll overlooking the creek.

"We hobble the horses up here," Odessa complained, "and them nighttime silhouettes will be mighty easy to spot."

Tap glanced through the evening shadows back at the brush along the creek. "If we leave 'em down in the thickets, the mosquitoes or the Indians will carry them off."

"You think there's Indians out here? I thought they all had to be back on the reservation."

"Leavin' horse bait would be one way to find out."

"You figure those two you ran off will double back for that reward money?"

"Not until they report to Shaver's Crossing.

But I do think we'll need to stand guard all night."

"You know," Odessa continued, "there might not be anyone after us nor any Indians in these hills. . . . You think maybe we're gettin' a mite distrustful in our old age?"

"Nope." Tap's reply rang with authority. "And we aren't old, Lorenzo."

"Shoot, Tap, how many of the boys we used to pal with are still alive?"

"They died young, that's all. I'll take the first watch."

Tap sat cross-legged in front of his saddle and stared through a darkening sky at the creek below. Soon all he could see were two shades of black and a blanket of stars. From time to time he could hear the horses whinny and shuffle their hobbled hooves.

There were no sounds of rustling wind.

No babbling brook.

No lonely coyote howl.

Nothing.

Tap calculated it must have been just past midnight when he observed a light flash in the distant western hills. His head was slumped on his chest as he leaned back against his saddle. His eyes blinked open as he waited for another flash.

One, two, three vertical and two silent horizontal ones. So far away I can't even hear the thunder.

Tap glanced up and could still see a canopy of stars.

This is crazy, Lord. I should just go home. What am I doin' chasin' down Cabe and Banner? I don't know for sure who shot Tracker. I don't know what went on back in the cedars, nor do I have any authority to do anything. Used to be I'd just trail after someone and do what I thought was right. But it always felt more like vengeance . . . or a grudge . . . or just a way to prove myself.

I guess I'm mainly mad. Mad at bein' slicked. Mad at myself for fallin' for that talk about runnin' a big ranch. Mad because I can't seem to find a peaceful job and leave my past behind.

Yep, I ought to just ride back to Pine Bluffs and forget Cabe.

That's what I ought to do.

In a couple nights I'd be in Pepper's arms instead of out here on the prairie.

"Is that storm headed this way?" Odessa's low, quiet voice broke the stillness and caused Tap to slip his hand onto the trigger of his rifle.

"Looks like it's kind of stuck on those hills."

"Grab yourself some sleep. I'll take a shift," Odessa offered.

It was too warm to crawl into a bedroll, so Tap leaned his head back on his saddle and closed his eyes.

At least I can rest a bit. Won't be able to sleep much. Too much flashin' through my mind. Too many plans. Too many disappointments. Too many . . .

The first crash of thunder sounded like an

explosion right above his head. Tap's eyes flew open. He rolled to his hands and knees when the second blast hit. It was raining hard, and his hands and knees hit mud. The blinding light revealed shadowy outlines of men standing in a circle not more than twenty feet from him.

Hard men.

Angry men.

Well-armed men.

The thunder rolled again. Someone fired a shot that ripped into his left leg. A sharp pain flashed up to his hip. Tap rolled in the mud and the dark and grabbed for his Colt, but the gun was missing. When he lurched to his knees, another flash of lightning revealed the men now only a few feet away. Rain streamed down his face and soaked clear through his shirt. He fumbled for his rifle, cocked it, and fired in the dark, but it wasn't loaded. Instead of a flash of gunfire, there were only laughs and curses.

Grasping his bullet belt, he couldn't find any cartridges at all. He clutched the rifle by the barrel and swung it wildly at the approaching men. Someone kicked his wrist, and he dropped the rifle in the mud. The rain continued to pour. The mud oozed between his fingers. The pain in his leg made him want to scream. A thick-legged man kicked his arms out from under him, and he fell facedown in the mud. He reached out for the swinging boots, but someone jammed a boot heel in his back and a cold, wet gun barrel into his ear.

"You're a dead man, Andrews!" a voice sneered.

The flashing lightning now revealed a crowd of at least a hundred angry men. He couldn't see any faces. Just boots and britches and gun barrels.

"Andrews, do you hear me?"

Tap struggled to keep his mouth out of the mud as he gasped for air.

Not here . . . not like this . . . I haven't even seen the baby, Lord. Not now!

"Andrews! Do you hear me?"

"I can't . . . ," he tried to mutter.

"Tap! Come on. Wake up!"

His eyes blinked open. A shadowy figure hovered above him. It wasn't raining, but his shirt was wringing wet. His left leg, twisted under the full weight of his body, ached. He pulled his Colt out of the holster.

"Tap! It's me — Odessa. You're only dreamin', partner! Relax."

Andrews sat straight up and peered through the darkness.

"It's only a dream."

"A what? Is it rainin'?"

"Nope. Come on, Tap, put that gun back. You're awake."

"Yeah . . . yeah . . . Lorenzo?"

"I'm here."

"I guess I sort of had a nightmare."

"That's a mild way of puttin' it."

"Is it still clear?"

"Yep."

"Then let's ride."

"It won't break daylight for a couple hours."

"I'm not in the mood to sleep."

"You ever pitched that horse at night?"

"Nope."

"Me either. I reckon we'll end up in the rocks or in the cactus."

"I'm pullin' out for Pine Bluffs, Odessa. You can stay, go, do whatever you want," Tap barked.

"Whoa, partner, what's happenin' here?"

"I've got to go check on Pepper. I'll turn a report in on Tracker, Cabe, and Banner. The sheriff can trace it down."

"What about that Texas herd?"

"You don't have to go with me, but I'm leavin'!" Tap growled. "You want to chase stolen cattle, go right ahead."

"Wait . . . wait. I didn't say I wasn't goin' with you. I just didn't figure you for quitting when the trail is still hot."

Tap stumbled to his feet and felt a deep, painful throb in his left leg. He had to struggle to keep from collapsing.

"Maybe we'll wait for daylight," he announced. "Let's fix some coffee."

"What about needin' to have a cold camp?"

"I need coffee worse."

"Yeah," Odessa replied, "maybe you do."

They didn't say more than two words to each other for the next hour as they huddled around a scroungy, little fire and sipped on coffee that had been boiled in their cups.

199

In the colorless morning light, Tap glanced over at Odessa. His eyes were closed, his left hand holding his tin coffee cup and his right hand on the grip of his .45. "Let's ride, partner," Tap announced.

Odessa sat up and tossed his cold coffee on the glowing coals of the campfire. "Where we headed?"

"Shaver's Crossing."

"But I thought you said you were goin' home."

"I think my memory just slipped a cog there in the night."

"That's a mild way of sayin' it." Lorenzo laughed. "For a while I figured I was going to have to shoot you before you shot me."

Tap left the hobbles on Roundhouse as he saddled up. "We've got to see if Cabe and Banner are at Shaver's. If they aren't, we might have to ride up Lone Tree Canyon."

"You figure out how we're goin' to take on a couple dozen men?"

"Nope. Are the Texicans with the herd drovers or gunfighters?"

"I hear Tracker got rid of his gunmen when they crossed into Colorado. Except for a couple of malo hombres, I hear he's got mainly a cowboy crew."

"Then all Banner has to do is ride over to that herd and jump the cowboys."

"Or pay them off. We need a better plan than we had at Runnin' Water."

"How did I know some drunken gambler was

goin' to take potshots at you?"

"I did like the way you got that man Owen to break my pony for me. Don't suppose he'd do that ever' time I mount, do you?"

Tap shook his head and laughed. "I don't know what's more stupid — you and that roan, or me and this gray."

"We're both so bullheaded no decent horse would put up with us."

✓✓An hour before daylight they reached the North Platte. The horses had protested the night ride, but both men managed to stay in the saddles. They made camp in the brush after they swam the horses across the river. A small fire dried their clothing. After a rest Tap and Lorenzo rode east until they could see Shaver's saloon/general store. There were no lights. Three horses stood asleep in the corral, but Tap couldn't make out much in the shadows.

"All right, Mr. Tapadera, what's the plan?"

"I go in the front door, and you go in the back."

"Oh, yeah, that's a great plan. We tried that last time, remember?" Odessa protested.

"Well," Tap drawled, "then how about me goin' in the back door, and you goin' in the front?"

"Now that's a good plan!" Odessa shook his head and grinned.

"You promise not to shoot anyone before I get in the building?" Tap quizzed.

"You promise not to dally around visitin' with the neighbors this time?" Odessa challenged.

"I'll be there. Only thing that bothers me . . . there's not many horses in that corral."

"You think they all left?"

"Maybe, but they might have left a few."

"What if the doors are braced?" Odessa asked.

"You too old and feeble to bust down a door?"

"Nope. I just don't want no surprises."

A bullet ripped bark from the cottonwood right next to Tap. At the same moment they heard the report, they saw the smoke from the gun barrel pointed at them from the front door. Both men dove behind the trees.

"You're right, partner. Don't worry about the front door. It's open." Odessa fired one shot into the thick wooden door and crouched back down.

"Which one of us was goin' to take the front door?" Tap joshed. "Take the bottom hinge. I'll take the top."

Both men fired off three quick shots. The big, thick wooden door tumbled off its hinges and into the store.

A voice echoed across the yard to the trees. "Wait! Don't shoot anymore!"

It was a woman's voice.

8

"Selena?"

"Tap?" Her voice sounded strong, yet on the verge of cracking. "Tap, is that you?"

"Selena, who's in there with you?"

"No one alive. Who's with you?" she called out, still not showing herself.

"A friend of mine — Lorenzo Odessa. Come on out."

"Why were you sneaking up on the store?"

"Why were you shootin' at us?"

"I thought you were them."

"Who?"

"Banner and Cabe and the others. I thought they had come back to kill me."

"Why would they do that? Aren't you and Banner . . . married?"

Selena stepped over the fallen door to the open doorway, her shoulders slumped, a trapper model '73 Winchester with a fifteen-inch barrel dangling from her left hand. Even from the trees across the yard, Tap could see that the sleeve of her dark dress was torn, her face smeared with dirt, her left eye black and blue.

"Would a husband do something like this?" She was now obviously struggling to hold back the tears. "You knew we weren't really married."

"He beat her up, Tap. I can't believe any man would do that!" Odessa raged.

203

Favoring his left leg, Tap hobbled across the yard, still carrying his rifle. "It's all right, darlin'. Come on, we'll get you out of here."

Selena dropped her short-barreled carbine on the front porch and met Tap at the bottom of the steps. Her face, neck, and arms showed signs of deep bruises. She didn't wait for him to invite her. She collapsed in his arms, clutching him tight.

"It's okay, darlin' . . . it's okay."

"I'll kill him. Whoever did this, I'll kill him!" Odessa exploded.

"Selena, this is Lorenzo Odessa — an old friend from my Arizona days. Was it Banner who did the punchin' on you?"

"Mainly."

"There were others?" Odessa questioned.

"You made 'em all mad, Tap. They took it out on me."

"I made 'em mad? What are you talkin' about?" He stroked her long, thick black hair with his hand.

"Why do men like to hit me, Tap? They always beat on me." Selena's dark eyes pleaded even more than her voice. "How come they never beat on Pepper? All the time we worked at April's, men would never slug her or nothin'. They always hit me."

"Why didn't you use your gun?" Tap asked.

"He took it away before I even knew he was mad. They held me down. I couldn't draw my knife." Selena sucked up the tears and tried to show a hardened determination.

Odessa stomped back and forth on the porch. "I'm goin' to kill the whole works! It ain't right, Tap. I'm goin' to kill 'em all!"

"Lorenzo, pick out the gentlest pony left in the corral and see if you can find a saddle. We're takin' Selena with us."

"She can ride with me," Odessa offered.

"Sure, you plan to put her on that blue roan and let her get bucked into the rocks?"

"You're right. I'll go get her a pony." He started toward the corrals and then turned back. "Miss Selena, I really am going to kill the hombre who did this."

Odessa stomped across the porch, spurs jingling. Tap sat Selena down on the step and then plopped down beside her.

"Who's inside dead?"

"I don't even know his name. The old man who runs the ferry was drinking at the bar and tried to stop them from beating on me. He shot him."

Tap let his black hat slide to his back, held on by the stampede string. "Who did?"

"That man Cabe. He shot the old man in the back."

Tap brushed his mustache and felt a week's stubble in his beard. "And you said I'm the cause of all this?"

"The other day when we saw you at Running Water, Banner was furious that I talked to you and invited you to eat with us. He punched me around pretty good that night. The next day he

205

spent drinking, and I stayed in the room upstairs. I didn't want to go out lookin' all beat up. He came back that night crying and drunk, promising to never hit me again."

"And you believed him?"

"If I'd had stage fare, I would have rode off as soon as I could. But I was stuck and figured I would last it out until we got back to Cheyenne or Denver. But the following day, this guy Cabe comes rambling in, spouting to everyone in the room that you shot his partner in the back and were trying to kill him. Then he and Banner got real private and worked out some kind of partnership on a big Texas herd."

"Cabe said that I killed Tracker?"

"I told Banner that Tap Andrews never shot a man in the back in his life. I called Cabe a liar and told Banner that he should have nothing to do with him."

"I don't suppose that sat well with Wes Cabe."

"No, and it made Banner mad, too. He slapped me down. I should have shot him right then. I knew I should have shot him. But Banner and Cabe had some plan cooking. Within an hour or so I found myself in the saddle riding off with the two of them for this place. I don't even know where I'm at! Banner left a couple men back at Running Water to keep an eye out for you, just in case you really tried to follow Cabe."

"Yeah, I had a run-in with them."

"You should have shot them."

"Why?"

"Well, we got here, and everyone was pretty much liquored up. Banner figured we'd spend the night here, then take the whole crew up to Lone Tree Canyon and pick up the others, then ride out to Nebraska and take over that Texas herd."

"What do they plan on doin' with them?"

"Drive them to Custer City and sell them off quick, I think."

"What happened here last night?"

"Well, the two from Running Water come riding in late to say that you're on the prowl. That makes them all pretty nervous. I guess they were hoping you were just goin' to go back to Pine Bluffs. Then in the middle of the night, another rider shows up from Running Water and says he tracked you in this direction, and you were asking around about me."

"Askin' about you?"

"Banner gets whiskey-drunk and really begins to whale on me. Some of the others give him a hand. That's when the ferryman gets killed. After a while I'm not movin', so they ease up and leave me alone. Banner and Cabe decide they should saddle up right then and ride to the canyon with the others. There's no way you could fight them there."

"He's probably right. Why didn't they take you?"

"Banner had this plan. He said if they left me here all beat up, you would call off the chase and take me to Cheyenne City or Pine Bluffs."

"Banner said that?"

"Yeah."

"He's right, you know."

Selena wiped her bruised eyes on her sleeve. "I know."

"Well, if you knew I was coming, why take shots at me?"

"I didn't see you. I just saw your friend . . ."

"Lorenzo."

"Yeah, Lorenzo. Some of them threatened to circle back and finish me off. I was afraid maybe it was them. I was scared, Tap. It was like that time you and Stack saved me from that bunch out at April's."

Tap glanced up. Odessa led a short black gelding around to the front of the store. "You want to wash up before we ride?"

"Where are we going?"

"I'm takin' you back to our house in Pine Bluffs. You can stay with me and Pepper. And Angelita."

"Who?"

"A little girl who's stayin' with us awhile."

"Pepper might not want me around."

"Listen, you two might fight like sisters, but you're family. All you girls are family, and you know it."

"Yeah." She sighed and stood to her feet. "Somehow I knew you'd say that." She started to walk back into the store. "What about this ferryboat man?"

"We'll bury him while you clean up."

"Tap, I don't even know his name! An honorable man died trying to help me, and I don't even know his name."

"The Lord knows his name. I got a pretty good idea he'll get a fair shake."

"You and Pepper still hangin' on to all that religion?"

"Yep. You ought to look into it yourself, Selena. I think you could find some comfort and forgiveness —"

"I don't need you preaching at me, and I surely don't need . . ." Her harsh tone cracked, and she stared at him with pained eyes. "Yeah . . . I do need that, don't I? Maybe I'd better talk to Pepper about it."

"It's not a game, Selena. God's really there. He really cares. I'm sure Pepper will be happy to talk to you."

Actually, Lord, I'm not all that sure Pepper will be happy to have another house guest . . . especially Selena. Maybe You could sort of prepare her for this. It surely would be appreciated.

Tap and Lorenzo brought the dead man's body out of the store. Finding a shovel in the back of the building, they buried him among the cottonwood trees.

Then they mounted and bucked their horses out before Selena returned to the yard.

"You mean they beat up Miss Selena because they knew that would throw you off their trail?" Odessa fumed.

"I reckon that's about it," Tap conceded. He

turned to Selena. "You ready to ride?"

"I'm ready to ride, shoot, stab . . . yeah, I'm ready," she replied. Her long, straight black hair had been combed and now hung down her back, almost to her narrow waist.

"Which direction, Tap?" Odessa asked.

"We'll head west back along the North Platte and then drop south of the Laramie River, picking up the Cheyenne-Deadwood road just below the Fort."

"That's kind of roundabout, ain't it?"

"I have no intention of riding into Lone Tree Canyon with Selena alongside. If we swing out to the east, we could run across the whole gang or that Texas herd — or both. It's safer this way."

"But that's exactly what they were hopin' we'd do," Lorenzo argued.

"Well, this time they're right. We'll spend the night at a roadhouse in Chug Water, then cross Little Bear Creek and swing back to Pine Bluffs, avoiding Cheyenne. It'll be quicker."

"Tap, I'm goin' after them right now," Odessa announced. "You take Miss Selena to your house. I'll track down Banner and Cabe."

"That's foolish, Lorenzo. One man can't take on the whole gang. Besides, you don't know where Lone Tree Canyon is, and you've never seen Cabe or Banner."

"It don't matter. I'll find them."

"It does matter. You'll get yourself killed."

Odessa trotted the blue roan on up ahead of them, then slowed down. "I could just trail them

210

until you join back up with me."

"Mr. Odessa, Tap's right," Selena broke in. "I appreciate your great concern for me. Truly I do. But one man I don't even know has already died trying to help me. I'd prefer that no others do. Besides, I feel safer with two escorts. Especially when they are both strong, handsome, and obviously quite handy . . . with a gun."

"Yes, ma'am." Odessa tipped his hat toward Selena. "Well, there you have it, Tapadera. We'll just both take her to Pine Bluffs."

Pepper didn't care if it rained. She was just getting tired of the dry thunder and lightning. Ever since she and Angelita had returned from Colorado, they sat on the porch every evening and watched empty clouds roar and crack their way across the prairie.

What she was really getting tired of was waiting for Tap.

He said he might be gone two weeks. Well, it's two weeks tomorrow, and I want him home. I don't know why I ever agreed to this. I told him when we moved to Pine Bluffs that I didn't want him having a job where he would be gone a lot. I wanted him home at night. I want to talk to him.

Lord, I want to talk to him right now.

Money. It was money, wasn't it?

We wanted that extra hundred dollars.

"It won't rain, you know." Angelita's soft soprano voice always sounded melodic. "It reminds me of Billy Sanchez. He always threatened to

211

punch me in the nose, but he never did. At first I was scared. Then I used to laugh and make fun of him. I think maybe Mr. Andrews will come home tonight. Do you think it will be tonight? It would be a good night for him to come. I can't wait to tell him that my father is getting better and . . . well, you know . . . that he's going to marry that woman. Look, I'm messing up again." She stared at the needlework in her lap. "I mess up every night. I don't think I will ever learn. Maybe God just doesn't want me to do domestic work."

"What does the Lord have to do with your ability to sew?" Pepper took the flour sack towel off the arm of her wooden rocking chair and wiped the perspiration off her forehead.

"He made me just like I am, right?"

"Yes."

"And you told me God never makes any mistakes."

"That's right."

"Well, I was thinking. Maybe He makes some ladies to do housework and cooking and sewing and all that. And then maybe He makes some other ladies with different skills and abilities."

"And I suppose you're one of those 'other' ladies?" Pepper laughed.

"That's obvious, isn't it? Look at this mess. A kitten with a ball of yarn could do better than this."

"Let me help you get it straightened out."

"Why? The same thing will happen tomorrow."

"Who knows," Pepper teased, "perhaps tomorrow the Lord will give you the patience to slow down and knit well."

"Slow down? I want to speed up. That's the main trouble with knitting. It takes such a long time. You know what else takes a long time?"

"What?"

"Growing up. It seems like I've been ten and three-quarters forever."

"Some seem to grow up faster than others." Pepper sighed, raising her eyebrows at Angelita.

"Well, I'm not growing nearly fast enough. How come all the good men are either married or too old?"

"What in the world are you talking about?"

"Well, Mr. Andrews is married, and Mr. Lowery is too old."

"Stack is too old for what?"

"To marry me. What do you think I'm talking about?"

"Oh, I'm sure there's some ten-and-three-quarters-year-old boy somewhere who's planning on owning a gold mine someday."

"Well, I'm not just going to wait around forever. . . . Which reminds me, you didn't answer my question."

"Just exactly what question didn't I answer?"

"Are we going to have to keep waiting, or is Mr. Andrews going to be home tonight?"

"Let's pray that the Lord brings him home safe tonight."

"You think God will answer that prayer?"

"He'll answer, all right."

"Then Mr. Andrews will be home tonight?"

"Perhaps. But that might not be the answer God gives us."

Pepper always thought outlaws and lawmen rode horses the same way. Carbine across the lap, straight back, suspicious eyes, no smile, determined gait, hat pulled low, stampede string tight, and topcoat brushed back behind the revolver.

The only difference was that outlaws, going longer between baths, were dirtier.

Usually.

The man who rode the tall sorrel stallion was definitely a lawman. Clean-shaven. Shirt and tie. Hat freshly blocked. Even on a hot, sultry night, he looked crisp and clean.

"Evenin', ma'am," he called out from horseback as he tipped his hat toward Pepper and Angelita.

"Good evening," Pepper replied.

"I'm lookin' for Tom Slaughter. The office was closed, and a fella pointed me toward your house sayin' you might know where I could find him."

"I believe Mr. Slaughter said he was going out to Nebraska to check on some Texas cows. I have no idea when he'll be back. Can we help you with anything?"

"No, ma'am. I just need some information about one of your Pine Bluffs residents, and Tom's the only one I knew in town."

"Are you a lawman, mister?" Angelita asked.

He grinned and nodded his head. "Guess that's kind of hard to disguise. I'm the new U.S. Marshal."

"Perhaps we can help you," Pepper suggested.

"Well, ma'am . . . it's not the kind of business to trouble you ladies over."

"Did someone get murdered?"

"Angelita!" Pepper scolded.

"Actually, yes, ma'am, they did."

"Who?" Pepper and Angelita echoed the same question.

"Without talkin' about any details, a man was shot in the back up in Crook County. I've got the arrest papers."

Pepper could feel a cramp in her stomach and the baby kicking. "Who got shot?"

"A Texas man. Goes by the name of Tracker. Jacob Tracker."

"Oh . . . my!" Pepper moaned. She could feel her heart sink.

Angelita stood up and walked to the front edge of the porch. "Who are you looking for?"

"I have arrest papers for a Mr. T. Andrews. You two don't happen to know where he lives, do you?"

No . . . no! Lord, he doesn't . . . Why can't we . . . Tap wouldn't . . . I just want us to be left alone, Lord. I didn't want him to . . .

"He lives right here, and he never shot anyone in the back in his life! Besides, he's not home!" Angelita thundered.

"Is that true, ma'am?"

215

Pepper nodded her head.

"Listen, I don't know anything about it except we have papers signed by a Wesley Cabe and a Colton Banner that say they saw Mr. Andrews shoot Tracker in the back. There'll be an inquiry, and if there's enough evidence, a fair trial. It would be best for him to give himself up when he comes home. I'll be over at the Railroad Hotel. If we have to track him down, we will. And chances would be mighty good he could get hurt."

"You couldn't take him with a dozen men," Angelita screamed. "He was a deputy over at Cheyenne City and stopped that whole Del Gatto gang almost single-handed!"

"Well, I'm new in the Territory, so I don't know about any of that. But I'll bring him in one way or another. Good day, ma'am."

Pepper's hands were shaking, and she could tell she was going to cry.

"Mr. Andrews didn't kill anyone," Angelita tried to reassure her.

"Angelita, I'm goin' to go lie down." Pepper struggled to her feet.

"Do you want me to go get Mrs. Rosser?"

"No, it's not time for the baby . . . yet. I think I just need to lie down. Can you close up the house for me after a while?"

"Do you want me to stay up and watch for Mr. Andrews?"

"Honey, that would be nice. Wake me up if I'm asleep, although I doubt if I can sleep."

Pepper didn't bother changing into her nightshirt but just lay on her back in the middle of the bed. She unfastened the top four buttons of her dress.

She felt very dizzy, and her vision blurred, so she kept her eyes closed. Within a few minutes Angelita tiptoed in and pulled off Pepper's high-top, lace-up black shoes.

Lord, I don't think I can take this. I'm worried day and night about losing the baby, and I'm worried about Tap. Lord, that's my whole life. It's like I get real close to everything I ever wanted in life, and then it slowly gets pulled away from me. It's not fair. I just want some peace and quiet . . . and that ranch of Stack's for Tap to run up in Montana.

I haven't even had a chance to tell him about that, and now he's wanted for murder. This can't be happening. Give me some rest. My heart feels like it's racing a mile a minute.

She was vaguely aware that Angelita pulled the wooden rocking chair into her room and sat down after mentioning something about it start-ing to rain. By then Pepper could tell that she had perspired clear through her dress.

The trouble with being happy, Lord, is that I'm scared to death of losing it. At least when I was miserable, things couldn't get any worse.

The path through the trees narrowed as it as-cended. Even though the tall firs and pines blocked most of the sunlight, the trail was lined with such thick brush that Pepper could see very little.

I've got to find him! He could be lost. He could be hurt. I've just got to find him!

Her long brown dress caught in the brambles, and when she tugged at it, the hem ripped. She stumbled over some fallen branches and twisted her right ankle.

I can't stop! I've got to find him. Why didn't I wear my shoes?

The mountain grew steeper, and Pepper had to stop often to rest. She stooped over and put her hands on her knees and tried to catch her breath.

"Tap! Do you hear me? Tap, where are you?"

The words bounced off the trees, but there was no reply.

A few yards farther up the trail, she could see a clearing where the sun was shining. Breaking into the little meadow, she again called out, "Tap? Please answer me, Tap!"

A few feet farther up the narrow path, she spied a tall, lone lodgepole pine in the meadow, standing like an arrow pointed to heaven. At the foot of the tree was a small wooden cross, the white paint cracked and faded.

"No!" she shouted. "No, Lord, no! Oh, please, dear God . . . not Tap!" Still a long way from the grave marker, she fell to her knees and began to weep. "I can't lose him, too. No, no, no!"

She struggled to her feet and staggered toward the marker. Several times she stumbled and fell. Her dress was covered with dirt, her hat fell off, and her long blonde hair flew in the wind.

"Tap," she sobbed. "Oh, Tap."

Falling down on her knees in the rocks in front of the grave marker, she wiped her eyes on the sleeve of her dress and shaded them from the bright noonday sun. She squinted to read the faded name on the cross.

Samantha Aimee Paige.

"Mother?" Pepper choked.

The tiny voice of an excited youngster sent chills down her back. "Mama!"

Still on her knees, she spun around. A four-year-old boy ran to her carrying two handfuls of flowers.

"Mama! Look at the pretty flowers!" he squealed.

"Tapadera Andrews, Jr., I've been searching all over for you!" she scolded.

"But, Mama, I told you I was going to put flowers on Grandma's grave. Look, I saved a bunch just for you!"

Laying one handful of purple, blue, orange, and red flowers in front of the white wooden cross, he handed her the others. Then he threw his chubby little arms around her neck and began to hug.

"Mama, I love you!"

Pepper began to cry.

And cry.

And cry.

She was sweating.

It was raining outside.

She hugged a pillow.

It was dark.

People were talking in the other room.

Someone was trying to shake her shoulder and wake her up. The voice was deep, strong, loving.

"Darlin'!"

Tap?

Pepper sat straight up in bed and groped about in the darkness. A muscular, callused hand slipped gently into hers.

"I'm right here, darlin'."

"Oh, Tap!" She reached out in the dark and found him, throwing her arms around his neck. "I just had a horrible dream."

"Again? The one about losing the little boy over the cliff?"

"No, no . . . it started out terrible but turned out to be wonderful. He was right there. He was okay. He hugged me and gave me flowers. . . . Oh, Tap, I'm so glad you're home! Turn on a light. Let me see you. I've got to talk to you!"

"Come on out to the living room. We've all got to talk. Pull on a robe. We've got company."

"I, eh, still have my dress on. Let me wash my face, and I'll be right out."

When she entered the room, Angelita was stoking the woodstove and boiling coffee. The air was hot and humid. Pepper could hear rain bounce off the shake roof. Tap tugged off a soaking wet ducking jacket and visited with a broad-shouldered blond man. A woman sat on the edge of the divan with a blanket around her shoulders, rocking back and forth.

"Tap, what's going on?" she managed to choke.

"Darlin', this is Lorenzo Odessa. My old-time friend from Arizona."

"You mean, all those 'Odessa-and-me' stories were true?"

"Most of 'em. I ran across him up at Sundance Mountain, and he's been helpin' me out."

"Who's the woman?" Just as she said that, the lady beneath the blanket looked up and stared into Pepper's eyes.

"Selena! But what . . . What's she . . ." Pepper looked back at the dark-haired woman one more time. "Selena, what happened to you, girl?"

Pepper swooped across the room and sat down on the couch next to Selena. She threw her arms around the blanketed woman's shoulders and hugged her tenderly. "Oh, honey, you aren't still working the dance halls, are you?"

Selena rocked back and forth in Pepper's arms, but didn't say anything.

"What happened?"

"Selena's been travelin' with Colton Banner. He's the one behind most of the cattle rustlin' around here. Well, me and Odessa were trailin' down that guy, Cabe, when he teams up with Banner. We're gettin' a little too close, and he decides it's Selena's fault, so he beats her bad and abandons her."

"Cabe and Banner? Tap, they had papers made out to arrest you for murdering Tracker!"

"I know. Angelita told me."

"What's this all about?"

"It's about one thief double-crossin' another thief, shootin' him in the back, and then teamin' up with Banner in order to take over a herd of stolen Texas cattle."

"I don't understand." Pepper finally realized how sloppy she must look. She released Selena and began to button up her dress. "What are we going to do?"

"Me and Odessa need to ride out east of town and see if we can locate that Texas herd. Chances are pretty good that Cabe, Banner, and a bunch of them will be headed this way."

"What will you do if you find them?"

"We'll stop 'em from takin' that herd north."

"But if you kill Cabe and Banner, how will you prove you're innocent of Tracker's murder?"

"Justice, darlin'. . . . We've got to see that justice is done. The Lord will have to take care of me."

"I don't want you to do this kind of work anymore," Pepper protested. "It's just like you marshaling. I'm sick with worry."

"Mrs. Andrews," Odessa broke in, "someone's got to make them pay for what they did to Miss Selena. Any man who treats a woman like that don't deserve to live. That's the code. There ain't no way we can let them get away with that."

He's blond, fair-skinned, but he sounds exactly like Tap. Where did he come from?

"Well, at least you can stay around until your

clothes dry and I fix you some supper . . . or breakfast." Pepper rose and walked to the stove.

"A cup of coffee is all we have time for. When daylight hits, that marshal will come snoopin' around again. Where did you say he was stayin'?"

"At the Railroad Hotel," Angelita replied. "But you don't have to worry about that Texas herd. I heard Mr. Slaughter say he was going over there to check them out."

Tap spun around and looked at Pepper. "Tom went out there by himself?"

"As far as I know. He wasn't expecting trouble."

"Well, he's going to find it. Snatch your coffee, Lorenzo. We've got to hit the trail."

"You got extra cartridges?"

"Grab a couple of boxes from that desk by the door." Tap turned back to Pepper. "Darlin', you're absolutely right. I'm tired of this, too. But I've got to go take care of Banner and Cabe and a stolen herd of Texas beef."

"Why?"

"Because it's my job."

"Your job to go get yourself killed?"

"My job to see that some very wicked men get stopped."

"Why you? You're just one person."

"Two of us. Maybe three if Tom's still alive."

"Two, three — you can't go up against a whole gang."

"Sure, we can. We're on the right side."

Pepper felt her throat tighten, her heart race.

"But you could get killed. Tap, don't take so many chances. You think the Lord appointed you to do away with all wickedness?"

"No," he said quietly. "Just this particular wickedness."

She looked through the flickering lantern light at his deep brown eyes.

He can't help himself, can he? No matter what job he has, he'll be driven to situations like this. I've always known that I'll be a young widow. I don't think I can take that. It's like running down a steep hill — you know the danger is up ahead, but there's nothing in the world you can do to stop it from happening.

"We've got to get on the trail, darlin'."

"I know."

"Angelita, you take good care of my Pepper."

"I will."

Pepper stood up and wrapped her arms around him. His shirt was damp, but she put her head on his shoulder anyway.

"Darlin'," he whispered, "I, eh . . . I hope you don't mind lookin' after Selena until we get back. I should have asked, but I just didn't know what else to do."

"Of course I'll take care of her. I would have been insulted if you had made any other arrangements."

His lips were cold and chapped as always, but Pepper still felt the fire that warmed her heart and kept her nights from ever being too lonely.

"Now go on . . . capture your rustlers. Earn

your three dollars a day."

Angelita handed him a small tin. "There's ham and cold biscuits in there."

"You're a sweetheart." He stooped down and gave her a tight squeeze.

"That's obvious to all who have met me," she quipped.

Pepper walked the men to the front door with Angelita trailing behind. Selena still slumped on the edge of the sofa. "Lorenzo, look after my Tap. He's got a lot waiting for him at home." She patted her well-rounded stomach and tried to smile.

"Yes, ma'am, I truly will. We both have a lot to come back for." He tipped his hat and glanced back into the living room. "Goodbye, Miss Selena."

The saddle was rain-drenched when Tap swung up on Roundhouse's back. He was grateful that neither horse bucked; both seemed restrained by the thunder, lightning, and rain. It was a warm rain, and, except for being soaked, they didn't find it that unpleasant. The occasional flashes of lightning lit the horizon ahead of them, reassuring Tap that they were on the right trail. They followed the railroad tracks east, crossed Spring Creek at the Nebraska line, and arrived at Bushnell Siding about daybreak.

The rain stopped abruptly, as if the heavenly canteen was empty. The wind began to pick up, driving off the clouds and chilling them in their water-soaked clothing.

"How far north do you think they are?" Odessa called out.

"Well, if they were here at the siding when I telegraphed, they could be anywhere between here and the North Platte."

"You reckon Cabe and Banner have reached them already?"

"Yep."

"What are we goin' to do when we find them?"

"Take the herd away and let you drive 'em back to Texas."

"I get Banner, Tap. He's goin' to pay for what he did to Miss Selena."

"Is this all just righteous indignation, or is there some romantic interest here, Lorenzo?"

"Maybe some of both, partner. Men like Banner and Cabe are cow dung caked on the boot heel of society. The quicker they're scraped off, the better everyone's life becomes."

"And?" Tap pressed.

"Shoot, Tap, under those bruises, she's one purdy woman. What do you know about her?"

"Well, she's a lot tougher than you might imagine. She's fiery and won't hesitate to use her tongue, her knife, or her sneak gun if she's given a chance. She worked the dance halls with Pepper and —"

"Your Pepper worked the hurdy-gurdies?"

"So what?" Tap challenged.

"No, no, compadre — no insult intended. I just figured she was from back east, the way she carries herself."

"She's changed a lot since she brought the Lord into her life."

"So have you, my friend."

"Maybe it's your turn now, Odessa."

"You just might be closer to the truth than you realize. But first I'm going to take care of Banner."

Even the previous night's downpour couldn't erase the tracks of 1,720 cattle. Since most herds were driven or shipped in and out of Pine Bluffs, Tap was confident they had found the right trail. The western Nebraska prairie consisted of rolling brown grass-covered hills with no bushes, trees, rocks, or houses — just a sea of short grass laid almost flat by the rain.

Clouds sailed quickly above them, racing shadows on the sunny prairie that soon became sultry and steaming. Tap's wet clothing dried quickly and then began to soak with sweat. Lorenzo Odessa reached the top of a large knoll before Tap and signaled him forward.

"What's up, Odessa?"

"A rider comin' this way."

"Where?" Tap stared off at the repetitive horizon.

"To the north. . . . He'll come over that third hill in a minute."

"Soldier? Lawman? Indian?"

"Couldn't tell. But by the way he was clutchin' leather, I can tell you one thing — he's definitely wounded."

9

"You hear that?" Odessa turned in the saddle and stared at Tap. His blond hair curled out from under his hat and over his ears.

The distant muted sound of gunfire filtered toward them as they waited for the rider to reappear.

"I reckon that means that Banner and Cabe caught up with the herd," Tap suggested. He pulled a couple of cartridges from his bullet belt and crammed them into the breech-loading magazine of the '73 rifle.

A black horse thundered south. The wet prairie offered no dust. The hatless rider leaned over the horse's neck, both hands clutching the saddle horn. Blood clotted thick on his shirt under his right arm.

Tap rode Roundhouse across the trail, blocking the rider. "Whoa, partner! You look like you need some help."

The thin man, with wide, drooping mustache and shaggy, dirty brown hair, jerked back on the reins and stopped the horse between Tap and Odessa. His left suspender had been ripped, cut, or shot, and it tailed out across his duckings.

"What's happening up there?" Odessa rode over and held the reins for the man, who again slumped forward in the saddle trying to catch his breath.

"It's a massacre," the man muttered.

Tap handed him a canteen. "Are you with that Texas herd?"

"Yeah."

Andrews pulled off his red bandanna, folded it up, and then handed it to the man. "Press this up against that wound with your underarm."

"Thanks, mister."

"You need to get to a doc in Pine Bluffs. Can you make it? You want one of us to take you to town?"

"I'll make it. I've got to get help for the others."

"What's going on?"

"We was movin' 'em on up to the North Platte when two dozen men came ridin' into camp at daybreak shootin' at anything that moved. We dove for refuge in some rocks just to save our lives, reckonin' that we didn't have much chance of keepin' the herd. But they came right at us. It was crazy. They acted like they wanted to kill ever' one of us. I don't even know who they are."

"How many of your men are left?"

"I don't know. . . . I saw a couple go down, but I don't know if they're dead. They'll be all right in the rocks until they run out of bullets."

"We'll go see if we can help out. Are you sure you can make it to town?"

"I'll make it."

"There's a U.S. Marshal staying at the Railroad Hotel. Tell him what's happened, and then tell him that Tap Andrews and Lorenzo Odessa went on out to help."

"You boys be careful. Don't get yourselves killed."

"We'll try not to, partner," Tap assured him.

"I'm much obliged for your help."

"You didn't see Tom Slaughter, did you?"

"Yeah. He rode up right before the shootin' started. I think he's one of the ones who took some lead."

"Go take care of yourself. We'll even the odds a little." Lorenzo handed the reins back to the man.

He and Tap spurred their horses north toward the sound of gunfire. Pulling up on a knoll, they peered across a smoke-filled basin.

"Do you think they're actually trying to kill them all off?" Odessa questioned.

"It looks that way. Didn't you say that's what they tried in Texas?"

"They're crazy."

Tap glanced over at Odessa. "Kind of sounds demonic, don't it?"

"Even the devil ain't that nasty."

"Don't underestimate him, my friend."

"Andrews, you sound like you figure ever' fight is a spiritual battle."

"It is."

Lorenzo Odessa shoved his hat back and shook his head. "I should have seen it comin'."

"What?"

"You gettin' religion. All those years we raised cain down on the border. You never were all that comfortable with sinnin'."

"Is anybody?"

Odessa nodded and rubbed the thin, blond stubble of his beard. "None but the likes of Banner and Cabe. How do you figure we'll do this?" He pointed up to the gunfight.

"Well, we can't ride down there and join those in the rocks. They're surrounded." Tap searched the horizon.

Lorenzo pointed to the southeast. "How about sittin' up there on that bluff to the west and catching a few in the cross-fire?"

"That might work. If we can do a little damage, maybe they'll just ride off with the herd and leave the Texicans alone."

Odessa stared Andrews down. "Do you believe that?"

"No, not really. You're right about the likes of Cabe and Banner. They seem to be kill-crazy. They won't stop until they're dead . . . or we are."

"I get Banner. Tap, you promised that I get Banner. I'm goin' to kill him."

"Partner, there's no room for mistakes today. Unbridled revenge has laid many a good man beneath the soil."

Odessa threw back his head and took a deep breath. "We can't sneak up on that bluff with the horses. They'll see us for sure."

Tap glanced around the prairie. "Well, there isn't a tree for miles. Let's hobble 'em and leave 'em here. Take all the bullets you can carry."

They hiked halfway up the bluff and then crawled on their hands and knees the rest of the way. Tap's chaps slid across the dead prairie grass as he dragged his left leg behind him. The bluff turned out to be an escarpment, with the south side a gentle grassy slope and the north a steep sandstone promontory.

Reaching the top, they peered through the smoke. Eight or nine cowboys were pinned down in rocks and boulders that weren't more than three feet high. Scattered around them, a dozen or more gunmen, finding cover where they could, pumped bullets into the rocks with such persuasion that the men under fire spent most of their time hunkered down, hoping to avoid a ricochet.

"Which ones are Banner and Cabe?" Odessa asked as he lay flat on his stomach.

"Can't tell. You see that bunch down there in that draw?"

"Yep."

"Let's try to flush them out. It might give those in the rocks a break." Tap checked the lever on his rifle, then flipped up the long-range sight, and began to raise the vertical adjustment.

"This carbine of mine won't do the damage that your rifle and peep sight can."

Propped up on his elbows, Tap pushed his hat to his back and took aim at the men on horseback in the draw, who were shooting into the rocks. "Shoot the horses."

Lying flat on the bluff, thirty feet above and two hundred yards away from the battle, Tap and Lorenzo opened fire. Twelve quick shots sounded before the smoke got so thick they had to cease firing.

A horse collapsed beneath the lead rider.

A second man tumbled from his mount.

A gray horse reared, bucked off its rider.

Another man slumped in the saddle.

The gunmen in the draw fled to the open prairie to face heavy shooting from the cowboys in the rocks.

"They'll try to flank us now," Odessa shouted as he and Tap hunkered down and reloaded.

"You watch the rear with that carbine. I'll keep some of them pinned down awhile."

"You think they're gettin' discouraged yet?" Odessa asked.

"Nope."

"Me neither."

"But maybe those in the rocks are feelin' a little better."

"You've got to tell me when you spot Banner."

"With all this gun smoke, I'm havin' a tough time tellin' a man from a horse, let alone finding Banner."

The prairie dirt on top of the bluff absorbed the bullets. The report from the guns was so rapid Tap couldn't tell how many were shooting back at them.

Lorenzo Odessa rolled over and shoved Tap down to a lower profile. "Them ain't bees buzzin', Tap."

"You hear bullets? I, eh, don't hear as good as I used to."

"You are gettin' old, Andrews!"

"No. It's just too many gun barrels bouncin'

233

off my head over the years."

"Same thing."

Tap peered over the bluff and cranked up the long-range sight to the highest notch. He aimed for a dark-colored horse whose rider pumped repeated shots into the rocks.

I hate shootin' good horseflesh, but I can't hit the rider from this distance. . . . Maybe they'll start thinkin' they're surrounded.

Just as Tap started to squeeze the trigger, Lorenzo's carbine blasted at a target behind them. Tap flinched at the explosion so close. The '73 Winchester lifted slightly higher than he had intended. His rifle blasted away, and the rider on the dark horse plunged to the rain-dampened prairie. The horse bolted away.

Tap didn't have time to follow his shot. He rolled to the right as Lorenzo rolled to the left, both men shooting back down the bluff as several riders approached from behind.

There's no cover! There's never any place to hide out here! Must have been what ol' Custer said up on the Little Big Horn.

Six riders charged up the gradual grassy slope of the bluff. Lorenzo winged the one who led on the left, and Tap plugged the one on the right. The other four spun their mounts and galloped back down the hill.

"Are they comin' back?" Odessa yelled from a cloud of white gun smoke.

Tap turned back and stared over the bluff. "Not those four! They're pullin' back."

Odessa crawled closer. "The whole bunch?"

"Yep. Looks like they're goin' after the herd."

"You figure they're givin' up on killin' everyone?"

Tap shoved more shells into the breech of his rifle. "Until they get a better plan, I reckon."

"We won't be able to hold on to this position if a bunch of 'em come chargin' up the backside again."

"Let's see if we can get those cowboys out of the rocks and headed south."

Odessa pulled several cartridges out of his vest pocket. "What about Cabe and Banner?"

"We can track them down with the herd."

"How we going to make it to the rocks?"

"Right down the bluff. They're too busy retreatin'."

"You're kiddin' me. That's almost a straight drop-off."

"Almost is not the same as a complete drop-off. We don't have time to make it to the horses."

"Andrews, you're as crazy as ever."

"Come on, Odessa. It isn't any worse than that time we rolled off into the Rio Grande."

"At least we were in a wagon that time."

"Only half the way down. Just don't drop your gun and have it shoot me in the back. Come on . . . we'll probably be able to walk all the way down."

Tap swung his legs over the bluff and dug his heels into the sandstone gravel. His rifle clutched in his right hand, he stood up and put his entire weight on his left foot. A sharp pain flashed up his leg to his hip. He stumbled, tried to catch himself, then tumbled to the gravel. Digging in his heels to stop the rapid descent, he instead somersaulted and rolled and bounced his way to the bottom of the cliff.

His left leg ached.

His right leg ached.

His arms ached.

His back ached.

His palms were rubbed raw and bleeding.

Tap rolled to his hands and knees and retrieved his hat. Shoving it on his head, he gasped for breath and glanced back up at Lorenzo. He was nowhere in sight.

He didn't come down! He's goin' down the backside!

On his first attempt to stand, he stumbled and fell on his face. Finally he was up on his feet and staggering toward the rocks. One of the cowboys ran out and offered his arm, leading him back to shelter.

"Where'd they shoot you?" he asked Tap.

Tap collapsed against a boulder, trying to catch his breath.

"I'm okay. . . . I just took a tumble tryin' to come down the cliff."

"You did that on purpose?"

"Eh . . . it didn't look so steep from the top."

Several of the men scooted over to Tap.

"I don't know who you are, mister, but all of

you up on the bluff are surely an answer to our prayers."

Another man scooted through the rocks toward them. "What are those bushwhackers doin' now?"

"They rode back to the herd. You boys got to get out of here and head south to the railroad tracks before they come back."

A man with a smear of blood on the right sleeve of his shirt crawled over to Tap. "We can't do that. We signed on to deliver this herd to Jacob Tracker up at Black Thunder Canyon. We ain't quitters."

"You the trail boss?"

"Yep."

"Well, I'm the one who sent you that telegram from Sundance Mountain. When I got back to Tracker, he'd been shot and killed. There's no one waitin' up there for you."

"Tracker's dead?"

"Me and Odessa buried him."

"But who's goin' to pay us? Who owns this herd now?"

"Folks back in Texas. This herd was stolen. Where'd all you boys hire on at?"

"Colorado, but we're all Texicans."

"You don't owe loyalty to any of these rustlers, boys. Tracker murdered some good Texans to steal this herd in the first place."

"What about our pay?"

"Right now you need to get out with your lives."

One of the wounded men looked up through pained eyes. "How do we know you ain't just tryin' to get us out in the open and then gun us down?"

"Tap?"

Andrews spun around. Tom Slaughter scooted over with a bandanna bandaging his shoulder. "What's goin' on here, Tap?"

"Tom! How bad is it?"

"I'll make it. What's happening here?"

"I think Tracker stole these cattle in Texas, hired these cowboys in Colorado, and intended to peddle the bovines off in the Black Hills this winter. As near as I can figure, Cabe double-crossed him, went in with a man named Banner, and came back to take the herd by force."

"They thought they could steal 2,000 head?" Slaughter asked.

"It's 1,720. They made it this far. We've got to get these men out of here before those rustlers get the courage to come back."

"We ain't been paid." A voice echoed an earlier concern.

"Tom, you think the stock association can pay these boys?"

"We'll cover your wages until we get this sorted out."

"Then why not consider the herd delivered, boys?" Tap advised. "Grab whatever ponies you can and ride south."

An older, dark-skinned man with a Mexican sombrero stood up and walked over to Andrews.

"I ain't leavin' the herd. I signed on to deliver 'em north of the Cheyenne River. That's where I'm takin' 'em."

"But there's no one there to take 'em when you get there."

The man reloaded his revolver from a nearly empty bullet belt. "Then we'll turn 'em out to pasture and go home. It's the principle. Ain't nobody ever goin' to say Sal Guzman didn't keep his end of the deal. I say we send the wounded back to Pine Bluffs, and the rest of us go after the herd. If they can steal it away, we can steal it back."

"Boys, I know how you feel, but the odds aren't good. How many do you have left to ride?"

"Eight of us can ride. How many you got up there on the bluff."

"Just me and Lorenzo Odessa."

"The two of you made all that commotion?"

"Yep."

"How many do they have left?" Guzman asked.

"Not more than twenty."

"I've been in worse fixes," the Texican asserted. He wore shotgun chaps with big silver conchos. "This time we can do the sneakin'. They ain't much in the way of drovers. I know we can out-cowboy them."

"Yeah, but they're bushwhackers and gunmen. Can you out-shoot 'em?"

"We've got to try. A man who loses a herd ain't worth spit."

"Sal's right," another man agreed. "Let's go

239

get our herd back."

Tap tried to brush all the dirt and debris off his chaps. "We'll ride with you if that's your decision," he offered.

"That makes ten of us," Guzman proclaimed. "I figure ten doin' what's proper ought to stand against twenty who ain't."

Horses were caught.

Wounded were tended.

Dead were strapped down on horses.

Guns were reloaded.

Bullets were handed over to those going after the herd.

Hoolihans were thrown. Hooves pranced. Latigos yanked tight. Spurs jingled. Saddle leather creaked. Within moments everyone was ready.

"I'm not going to be of much use to you," Tom Slaughter admitted.

"You lead the boys back. Wire the Tobblers in Texas and make sure this herd belongs to them. And tell that marshal where I'm at. Tell him I'm comin' to clear things up as soon as we get this herd back."

"You got trouble with a U.S. Marshal?"

"Yeah. I hear the marshal claims Cabe and Banner signed a warrant accusin' me of shootin' Tracker in the back."

"Is he serious?"

"Pepper seemed to think so."

"You want me to tell Mrs. Andrews anything?" Slaughter asked.

"Tell her not to worry. I've got everything

right where I want it."

"And that's supposed to comfort her?"

"She'll know what I mean."

One of the men led Roundhouse back to the rocks to Tap.

"Where's Lorenzo?" Tap asked.

"Your partner?" He waved his arm in a western direction. "Didn't see nothin' but some tracks buckin' their way over toward the buttes."

He's gone after them on his own! And I thought these drovers were crazy. Odessa might be the craziest Texican of them all.

With aches and pains in almost every part of his body, Tap tightened the cinch on Round-house and slipped his rifle back into the scabbard. Then he grabbed the horn and shoved his throbbing left foot into the stirrup.

Oh, no! I can't believe I mounted from the left . . .

Roundhouse bucked his hind hooves toward the clouds, then spun to the left. Tap couldn't get his right foot into the stirrup, but he managed to keep one hand on the reins and the other clutching a handful of mane. The tall gray horse bucked across the prairie with Tap hanging on at each painful bounce.

Finally finding the right stirrup, he spun the horse to the left, then to the right, and then raced him toward the place where he and Lorenzo had left the horses picketed earlier. He didn't dare look back at the Texas cowboys, but he could imagine the smiles on their battle-weary faces.

He quickly picked up Odessa's trail in the wet

soil. Lorenzo seemed to be following the high line north.

He's keeping the roll of the prairie between himself and the herd. Ridin' hard. Tryin' to get north of 'em, I surmise. He surely has taken to settlin' Selena's score. Lorenzo and Selena? Lord, how many battles and fights have been generated by love? Or, at least, lust?

Leading the others west, Tap soon signaled for them to wait up. Then he eased Roundhouse up the hill just far enough to peek over at the herd of cattle. They were being driven west into Wyoming Territory.

He led the cowboys in a circle farther west and came to two rocky buttes that marked both the trail into Wyoming and the Nebraska state line. The herd was still a mile away.

"You reckon we ought to take 'em during the daylight?" Guzman questioned.

"Nope. Let's swing out ahead and try to figure out where they'll bed down. The herd's too big to stop just anywhere. They'll have extra night guard, but they'll probably be lookin' to the south and east. We'll hit them from the northwest."

"Then why are we stoppin' at these buttes?"

"To pick up my partner."

"I see the blue roan . . . but where is he?" Guzman stood in the stirrups on his paint stallion and surveyed the boulders. His big Spanish rowels reflected the light of the sun, his eyes the boldness of twenty years on the trail.

"He's up there." Tap rode over to the base of

the rocks. "Lorenzo!" he called out.

There was a slight ruffle of wind and the sound of frisky ponies dancing.

"Lorenzo!" Tap hollered again.

"I'm goin' to kill him, Tap!" a voice filtered down from the rocks.

"We're goin' to get the herd back first."

"Then we're goin' to kill him?" Odessa shouted, still in concealment.

"Well, we'll make sure he gets what he deserves!"

"Okay . . . I'm coming down." Out of the top of the butte, Lorenzo Odessa scampered across the rocks toward the blue roan.

"Who does he want to kill anyway?" Guzman asked.

"Banner."

"Which one's he?"

"Wears a white shirt and dark tie — short man, weak-shouldered."

"I don't remember seein' anyone like that," Sal commented.

"He wouldn't be out in the lead. He's in the background makin' decisions."

Odessa pulled up into the saddle. The blue roan bucked for a dozen jumps before he settled down.

Guzman roared, "You two always ride unbroke horses?"

"Any fool kid can ride a broke horse. What's the fun in that?" Tap countered.

"Where we headed?" Odessa asked, once he got the horse under control.

"If you were a bunch of rustlers and bush-whackers drivin' cattle north, where would you want to cross the North Platte?" Tap prodded.

Odessa cinched up his stampede string and rubbed the dust from the creases around his eyes. "Somewhere shallow, easy to cross, not too close to Ft. Laramie . . . and knowin' that bunch, probably near a good supply of belly-churnin' whiskey."

"Sounds like Shaver's Crossing."

"You figure they'll ride right back to that saloon?"

"That's what I surmise. Only we'll get there first and set a trap."

"Twenty men and 1,700 bovines and . . . It's got to be a really big trap."

"Oh, it will be. Trust me." Tap spurred Roundhouse and led the band north.

It took the gunmen four hours late the next day to push the cattle across the North Platte. From Tap's vantage point in the brush on the north side of the river, he calculated that they lost half a dozen head and at least one horse in the water.

They aren't cowboys. That river's runnin' low.

He glanced back at Odessa and the others behind him.

Now if ever'one will wait, and if ever'one remembers, and if no pilgrims come wanderin' through, and if Odessa doesn't go crazy . . . Lord, that's a lot of ifs.

They didn't talk.

They didn't move.

They didn't smoke.

They just waited.

They waited until it got dark.

Then they waited some more.

The evening was warm and sultry with high, fast-moving clouds temporarily blocking the starlight.

It's easier to do at night, but a whole lot tougher to see if ever'thing is goin' right.

After hearing four gunmen load up on the ferry and head back across the river, Tap gathered the Texas cowboy crew.

"How many are left with the herd?" he asked Sal.

"Only four."

"Are they ridin' circle?"

"Yep. They seem to be the only four cowhands among the bunch." Guzman took off his sombrero and ran his fingers through his thick, gray-flecked hair.

Tap hunkered closer to the trail boss. "Can you 'Annie Laurie' 'em?"

"We'll take 'em."

"Without firin' a shot?"

"Yep."

"How many men do you need?" Tap asked.

"Me and four others."

"Okay, you take your crew and go at it. The rest of us will guard the crossin' in case you aren't as quiet as you think. We'll stop anyone who comes at the river."

"It was nice of them to ferry the wagons across," Odessa added.

"I suspect after two days they figured that no one was chasing them. Besides, if anyone came after them, they would expect it to be from the south, and that way they've got ever'thing across the river but their escape horses."

Tap spread Odessa and the other three Texans along the ferry landing and then positioned himself at the dock. Staring across the river in the dark, he watched the light beaming out the front doorway of the saloon. Banner and Cabe had not bothered replacing the door.

An occasional shout or laugh filtered over the slow-moving water of the North Platte. Behind him Tap could barely hear Guzman and the others begin their ploy.

> " 'Maxwellton braes are bonnie,
> where early falls the dew,
> And it's there that Annie Laurie,
> gave me her promise true.' "

Somewhere on the circumference of the herd, a startled rustler was listening to Salvador Guzman's melodic voice and greeting the barrel of a carbine with his forehead.

> " 'Gave me her promise true,
> which ne'er forgot will be;
> And for bonnie Annie Laurie,

I'd lay me down and die.' "

The lines were repeated over and over and over.

" 'Her brow is like the snowdrift,
  her neck is like the swan;
Her face it is the fairest
  that e'er the sun shone on.' "

Tap tried to imagine the shocked look on the night guards' faces as it dawned on them that the familiar words were part of a trap.

" 'That e'er the sun shone on,
  and dark blue is her eye,
And for bonnie Annie Laurie,
  I'd lay me down and die.' "

An hour later Guzman walked his horse to the ferry dock. In a voice that was little more than a whisper, he reported, "We've got the herd back."

"The night herders?"

"Tied and tossed by the river. They'll have some grand headaches tomorrow."

"As soon as your partners bring the horses across, get the herd up and start movin' them north. After that, Sal, you're on your own."

"*Gracias*, Andrews. It was real important for us not to lose the herd."

"I know. I'd have done the same thing if I were

you. I'll send a telegraph to Sundance Mountain to give you instructions on the herd. We'll contact Texas and get this figured out. They might want you to sell the whole lot."

"Do you think they'll follow?" Guzman pointed across the river.

"Not if we can pirate their horses. We'll cut that ferry loose and let it drift. They'll have to swim the river and pursue on foot. I reckon they'd want no part of that."

"Andrews, you'll do to ride the river with."

"And you as well, Sal."

Guzman tipped his sombrero, then mounted his horse, and rode back to the herd. Andrews gathered the other three Texas drovers and Odessa. While the Texicans rode, Tap and Lorenzo walked their ponies out into the middle of the river and then mounted. As they expected, neither horse bucked.

With the three drovers standing watch at the saloon, which was a couple hundred yards from the ferry landing, Andrews and Odessa sawed through the tie ropes on the big raft ferry and shoved it away from the dock. It began a slow drift into Nebraska.

"So far we're drawin' a good hand," Odessa whispered. "But remember, if Banner shows up outside that building, I'm going to kill him."

"You mean, if he shows up shootin' at us," Tap corrected.

"Eh . . . yeah. That's what I mean . . . sort of."

Tap signaled the drovers to circle to the back of the building near the corrals. All the horses were corralled, and all were still saddled. He and Lorenzo tied their own horses in the thick brush by the river and crept up to the log in front of the saloon where they had been only a few days before.

"There's no door to shoot off this time."

"Maybe they'll be able to take the horses without stirrin' up those inside."

"Do you believe that?" Lorenzo questioned.

"Nope."

The drovers had the corral gates open and were pushing the first horses out on the prairie. Suddenly someone ran out the front doorway shouting.

The 200-grain bullet from Tap's '73 shattered the porch post. The man dove back inside. A barrage of gunfire flew from the building. Tap and Lorenzo hunkered low behind the two-and-a-half-foot fallen log, not bothering to return fire until there was a lull. Odessa raised up, fired two quick shots through the open doorway, and then ducked down. Another stream of bullets bounced around them. Tap crawled on his stomach to the end of the log and watched through the dark night as the three drovers pushed the frightened saddle horses into the river. Several men on foot began to give chase, but a couple of shots from Tap's rifle sent them scrambling back to the safety of the building.

"They got the horses across," Tap announced.

"They're comin' into the yard now," Odessa noted. "They'll get us surrounded pretty soon. Are we goin' to charge 'em?"

"Give Sal time to get the herd moving. They have to chase those saddle horses into the hills before abandoning them. Let's crawl up there." He motioned to the clump of cottonwood tree stumps in the middle of the dirt yard. Keeping low, they scurried through the dark to the shelter of the four-foot-high stumps.

"Do you see Cabe or Banner?" Odessa prodded.

"No, but I wouldn't expect them to take any chances. Don't shoot into the building. Let's see what this bunch does."

"Don't you . . ." Tap put his finger to his lips to signal for silence. He and Odessa kept their guns pointed toward the saloon as they listened.

"How many are out there?"

"A dozen or more."

"They stole the horses. Did you get a look at them? Was it them drovers?"

"Them drovers is too scared to trail us. This here was Sioux or Cheyenne."

They think we're Indians? Maybe that will keep them inside. This is even better than my plan.

"How do we know they ain't surrounded the place?"

"They just wanted them horses."

"Banner told you to set a guard on the horses."

"Banner ain't here, and I was thirsty!"

Odessa started to say something, but Tap waved him off.

"You think they'll attack the herd?"

"I ain't heard no shootin' over there. I reckon they chased the horses off to Nebrasky."

"Someone's got to go after Banner and Cabe and tell them what happened."

They're both gone?

"Well, we ain't got no horses, it's pitch-black, and we're probably surrounded by bloodthirsty Injuns. . . . I ain't going out there until daylight. Maybe one of you wants to ferry across in the dark and drive back the rest of the remuda."

"Banner will kill us if we lose that herd."

"Banner can go to hades. I ain't steppin' out there. He's crazy. Both of them are crazy. They beat her up, and now they're goin' after her just to get even? I don't mind shootin' a man in the back, but I don't like the way they go after women."

Going after women?

A fist-sized knot seized Tap's stomach. He glanced over at Odessa, who didn't look back but just stared at the door.

"They can ride into Pine Bluffs and take hostages if they want, but I'm about ready to pull my picket pin and go to Montana."

"Yeah, me, too!"

"But we ain't got no picket pins, and we ain't got no horses."

"Well, in that case . . . we might as well drink!"

Without saying a word, Tap and Odessa crawled back into the brush and untied their horses. Silently they led them around to the west of the saloon and far out into the prairie.

"They went after Selena?" Odessa spat out as he tightened the cinch.

"And Pepper. Cabe knows who Pepper is and where we live," Tap added.

"Why? Why go after the women?"

"To flush us out in the open, I reckon. They want to force a showdown."

"They're goin' to get it, aren't they?" Odessa nodded.

"Yep."

Tapadera Andrews and Lorenzo Odessa bucked their way south into the dark prairie night.

10

Pepper slept until after 8:00 the next morning. She remembered Angelita crawling out of bed about daylight, but after that she recalled nothing.

The coffee was boiling, and a plate piled high with huge cinnamon rolls waited on the table when she finally waddled into the living room in her robe, combing her long blonde hair.

"I slept in," she said to Angelita's piercing big brown eyes.

"It's okay. You were tired. That marshal came by this morning."

"Already?"

"Yes, but I told him we didn't know where Mr. Andrews is or when he is returning."

"What did he say?"

"He said he'd wait. He said a man who has a baby coming any day now would surely be home soon."

"Any day now? What does he mean, any day now? It's ten weeks before my time!"

"Yeah, I told him that."

"Where's Selena?"

Angelita pointed to the back room. "She's still asleep in my bed. I think she was even more tired than you. I guess she's been in stormy weather for the last two days."

"She's been in stormy weather for most of her life." Pepper examined the rolls. "Where did these come from?" The room, normally filled with the stale smell of summer, now reeked of cinnamon.

"I picked them up at the bakery this morning."

"What do you mean, picked them up? You bought them?" Pepper questioned.

"Sort of." Angelita shrugged.

"Sort of?"

"Well, I traded for them."

Pepper stopped combing her hair. "You what?"

"I went down to the train depot and —"

"Oh, no. Angelita, you didn't . . ."

"I had my sewing project —"

"The baby mittens you're knitting?"

"Yes, well . . . I wanted to let you sleep, so I went down to the depot. And this lady gets off the westbound and looks at me and says, 'My, what an exquisite example of a primitive doily.' "

"A doily?"

"Then she says, 'Hubert, see if this little Indian girl will trade you for it. Don't offer her money. I hear it insults them.' "

"Indian girl? Money insults them?"

Angelita rocked back and forth on her black lace-up shoes. "She offered to trade me a little brass hand mirror, so I said, 'Sure.' Those mittens were a mess anyway."

"So you got a mirror?"

"Yes, but what do I need with another mirror? We all know how cute I look."

"So you traded the mirror for a plate of cinnamon rolls?"

"Three plates. We get one plate every day for three days."

Pepper reached over and held Angelita's warm brown hands. "Sometimes you completely amaze me."

"I even amaze myself. You know, I don't think I've ever met someone like me before." She dropped Pepper's hands and grabbed a big gooey cinnamon roll and sank her teeth into it. "You want me to go wake up Selena?" she mumbled.

"No, let her sleep. I've got some things to figure out first."

"Is she going to stay with us awhile?"

"That's one of the things I've got to figure out."

Selena made a bruised appearance about noon. The three spent most of the afternoon and evening, lounging in the shade of the front porch discussing friends and enemies, good times and bad.

The next morning Selena wandered into the front room where Pepper and Angelita were reading the Bible.

" 'Blessed is the man that walketh not in the counsel of the ungodly, nor standeth in the way of sinners, nor sitteth in the seat of the scornful. But his delight is in the law of the Lord; and in his law doth he —' "

"What's this word?" Angelita held the black book up to Pepper.

"Meditate."

Pepper glanced up at Selena but said to Angelita, "Go on. Finish reading."

Clearing her throat, Angelita took a deep breath.

" '. . . *meditate day and night. And he shall be like a tree planted by the rivers of water, that* bringeth forth his fruit in his season; his leaf also shall not wither; and whatsoever be doeth shall *prosper.* The ungodly are not so: but are like the chaff which the wind driveth away. *Therefore the ungodly shall not stand in the judgment, nor sinners in the congregation of the right*eous. *For the Lord knoweth the way of the righteous: but the way of the ungodly shall perish.' "*

"You take that all pretty serious now, don't you?" Selena asked.

Pepper studied Selena's battered, sad eyes and her beautiful flowing black hair.

"We're trying to learn. I've changed a lot in the past year," Pepper admitted.

"You're sure not the same woman I used to know at April's."

"Is that good or bad?" Angelita asked.

Selena burst out in deep laughter. "I envied the way the men always headed straight for you when they walked in the front door of April's. I hated you and would have liked nothing better than to bury my knife in that scrawny chest of yours a year ago."

Angelita's round eyes grew even bigger. "Really?"

" 'Course, I was probably drunk and sipping morphine at the time."

"Really?" Angelita gasped again.

"What about now?" Pepper asked.

"I still envy you. You pulled yourself out of that mess. You've got a home, a husband, a family. Even if you did have to lie and cheat and deceive to land him." A wry smile crept across Selena's face.

"Really?" Angelita's mouth dropped again.

Pepper looked over at her. "Don't you want to go down to the depot? I think the eastbound's due in soon."

"Are you kidding?" Angelita protested. "I don't want to miss one word of this."

She didn't.

Pepper talked of Tap, the coming baby, their dreams of a ranch, her constant fear of his getting shot, and her recently acquired faith in Christ Jesus.

By evening the topic of conversation turned to Selena.

"If you could lend me the money to take the train to Denver, I'd get a job and repay you," Selena suggested.

"I'm sure that would be fine," Pepper replied

as all three sat on the front porch. "But you won't want to leave before those bruises heal a little. Stay a few days."

"Thanks. I'd really like to wait and visit with Mr. Odessa again. Do you know anything about him?"

Pepper thought she noticed a slight twinkle in Selena's eyes and a blush on her cheeks. "No, I never met him before. But Tap's told me all about how they used to live it up down on the Mexican border."

"So he's pretty wild?"

"No more than Tap used to be. Tap hasn't seen him in a couple years. Sometimes men change."

"And sometimes they never do." Selena gingerly rubbed her bruised face.

"Why did that man Banner hit you, Miss Selena?" Angelita asked.

"Some men just like to beat on women, honey. What else can I say?" Selena glanced at Pepper for help.

"Dance halls are not very good places to work," Pepper explained. "Sometimes you see men and women at their worst."

Selena leaned her head back and closed her eyes, even as she continued to pull a large white brush through her hair. "Angelita, I've spent the last ten years trying to get rich men to like me and take care of me. Sometimes I wish . . . I wish I'd spent those ten years trying to get a gentleman to take care of me. A man can own the biggest gold mine in the Rockies and still be a fool."

"Really?"

Pepper glanced over at Angelita's wide-eyed expression. "She wasn't talking about Stack Lowery, of course."

A bandaged Tom Slaughter called on Pepper before dark. He reported the events of the previous day. "I've notified the authorities in Texas, Cheyenne, and Ft. Laramie. I'm on my way back out of town with a posse of fifteen men to assist Tap and the others up on the North Platte. Don't you worry, Mrs. Andrews. Ol' Tap told me to tell you he has ever'thing under control."

She stood on the porch with Angelita at her side. Selena was in the open doorway. The hot August breeze chapped Pepper's lips. Her skin felt very dry.

Everything under control? If it were under control, he would be home! What he meant was, tell her I'm doing those things that I can't keep myself from doing. Like chasing wicked men. Having guns fired at me at close range. Galloping off into the dark. Thriving on living on the edge of death.

Everything under control!

Tapadera Andrews, you have nothing under control!

You wouldn't have it any other way.

Pepper was surprised that the U.S. Marshal didn't ride out with Tom Slaughter but seemed content to sit on the front porch of a vacant house across the street and spy out her every move.

She was even more surprised when she went to bed early that evening that she actually went quickly to sleep.

The violent knocking at the front door brought Pepper to her feet even before she opened her eyes. She padded across the living room in the dark. A flicker from a light behind her caused her to look back. Angelita clutched a candle. Selena stood guard at the kitchen doorway, a carving knife in her hand.

"Who's there?" Pepper called out.

"Your husband's over at the livery, and he's bleedin' bad!"

"Tap's hurt?"

"Yes, ma'am."

"I'll be right there," she called. "Go get a doctor!"

"I reckon it's too late for that."

Angelita started to cry. Selena rushed to Pepper's side.

"I'll be right out. I must get dressed."

"You'd better hurry if you expect to talk to him," the man on the porch shouted out.

"O God, our help in ages past, our hope for years to come, our shelter from the stormy blast, and our eternal home!" The lines from the ancient hymn ran through her mind as she rushed back into the bedroom and began to dress.

"It's going to be all right, Angelita. The Lord

will take care of Tap . . . and us."

"He's going to die, and I'm goin' to have to go live with that lady and her five ratty kids!" Angelita wailed.

"Don't be silly. If anything happened to Tap, I'd need you all the more."

Angelita sniffled and wiped her nose on her nightshirt. "You would, wouldn't you?" She carried Pepper's shoes over to her, helped her put them on, and began to lace them up. "Aren't you scared, Mrs. Andrews?"

"I'm scared and peaceful at the same time. I don't know if I'm just in shock or if it's God's special grace for me. Either way, we'll just have to trust Him, won't we?"

"Yes, ma'am."

Selena appeared at the bedroom door, fully dressed, her long black hair flowing down her back.

Pepper pulled a knit shawl across her shoulders.

"I'm going with you," Selena announced. "I'm amazed that you can act so calmly."

"So am I. The baby isn't even doing the splits."

"The splits?" Selena asked.

"Oh, sometimes he seems to kick both sides of my stomach at the same time. But not now. He's real peaceful. It's like the Lord is saying, 'You can handle this, Pepper girl.' . . . Are you ready?"

"I'm staying right here. I don't like it when people I love get hurt a whole bunch," Angelita declared.

"Should we take a gun?" Selena asked.

"What on earth for?" Pepper walked over to the front door and put her hand on the latch. "Someday I expect to go and find Tap dead. I've always known that. But it won't be tonight."

"How can you say that?" Selena quizzed as she scurried to Pepper's side.

"Because he said he had it under control, and I believe him."

Pepper looked back across the room. "This is a crazy night. . . . Angelita, lock the door behind us."

"And I'll pray for Mr. Andrews."

"Pray for all of us," Selena added.

The dark shadows on the front porch flickered from the unsteady light of the lantern. To the south a dog barked. Up above stars glimmered. A distant sound of hoofbeats rolled up the street. The worn wooden porch floor creaked a bit as they descended the steps.

"Hello!" she called. "We're ready to go!"

It was like a winter squall.

A sharp, brisk chill slid from the nape of her neck down her spine and shuddered at her tail-bone.

No words.

No sight.

No hints.

Just an inner feeling — followed up by a deep, hate-filled voice. "Two birds in one trap. Cain't do any better than that!"

Selena spun around first. "Banner, you . . ."

262

"Mr. Cabe?" Pepper strained to see the man holding the shotgun on them. "Mr. Cabe, what is the meaning of this? I was told my husband was seriously wounded."

"Oh, he will be, ma'am. I guarantee he will be."

"You mean, Tap's not hurt at all? You used this ruse to get us out of the house?" Selena snapped.

"It worked, didn't it? Come on, ladies, we're going for a little walk."

"We aren't going anywhere!" Selena protested.

Colton Banner raised his revolver to strike her with the barrel.

Selena pulled a knife with a six-inch blade out of the sleeve of her dress and waved Banner back.

"You don't have ten men to hold me down this time, Banner!" she growled.

He pointed the revolver at her head and yanked back the hammer. "It only takes one bullet to stop you!"

"Then you better pull the trigger. You might kill me, but you aren't ever going to beat on me again! There are worse things than dying!"

"He won't shoot you, Selena," Pepper interjected.

"Why not?" he growled.

"Because if you merely wanted to shoot us, you'd have done that the moment we walked out into the yard. I presume you think that keeping us alive for a while will help you bushwhack my husband."

"She's right, Banner. Back off," Cabe cautioned.

"I'll do what I want with this woman!" Banner shouted.

"Not until we do away with Andrews and the other one," Cabe insisted. "Start walking toward the livery."

"Not when you use that tone of voice!" Pepper challenged.

"You're crazy, lady! Get movin', or we'll shoot you!" Cabe's voice cracked with anger.

Neither woman moved.

"Please!" he shouted.

"That's better."

Pepper had always assumed that Pine Bluffs had some nighttime activity, much like Cheyenne, only on a smaller scale. She was disheartened to discover that not one light was on, that not one person stirred in the entire town.

Where's that U.S. Marshal now? I heard hoofbeats. Surely someone will see us.

Selena refused to surrender her knife and returned it to her sleeve and walked on the right side of Pepper. She felt Selena's left hand slip into her right arm. Pepper squeezed it.

Banner led the way down the silent dirt street to the livery. He carried his revolver in his right hand. Wesley Cabe marched behind them with the short double-barreled shotgun pointed at the women. As they approached the big double doors of the livery barn, Pepper halted with a glance at Selena.

264

"Keep movin'!" Cabe growled.

"Shut up!" Selena barked. "Can't you see this woman's pregnant? She needs to catch her breath."

"After we do away with Andrews and the other one, you'll get the beatin' of your life!" Banner threatened.

"Selena, doesn't this remind you of the old days?" Pepper remarked.

"I said, keep movin'." A prod from the shotgun barrel forced Pepper to stagger forward one step.

Selena ambled a few steps. "You mean, like the time Tiny Moss and that bunch marched us out of April's across the street to the barn?"

"Yes. I think this is just the same, don't you?"

"I remember. But are you sure, Pepper girl?" Selena whispered. "You're in different shape than you were then."

"Fat girls can fight, too," came the muffled reply. "Let's do it!"

Before daylight Tap and Lorenzo stopped to rest the horses and take a nap.

"At the rate we're pushin' 'em, these cayuses ought either to be broke or dead by the time we get to Pine Bluffs," Tap remarked as he pulled the saddle off Roundhouse.

"I've been thinkin' the same thing. What I can't figure is, how in the world did the two of us fine experienced gunmen get stuck with these mounts in the first place?" Odessa grinned as he resat his hat.

"Because we're too pigheaded stubborn to admit we bought lousy horses."

"When we get back to town, I'll shoot your horse if you'll shoot mine. Then we'll have an excuse for buyin' new ones," Lorenzo offered.

Tap stretched out on top his bedroll. "You know what I can't figure? Cabe and Banner seem to be one jump ahead of us. They keep drawin' us away from the herd and the others. They seem to know what we'll do in every situation. Are we that predictable?"

"Yep. But we ain't never goin' to change. It gives us a sense of purpose."

"You mean, lookin' after women?"

Odessa plopped down on the dry prairie grass and propped his head on his saddle. "I mean, lookin' after women, children, and all those others who can't look after themselves. If we didn't do that, we'd be saddle bums like the ones we're chasin'. It's the thing that separates us from them. There has to be somethin'. Because you and me know we aren't like them . . . deep down inside, at least. We don't even think the same. Know what I mean?"

"Lorenzo Odessa, cowboy philosopher."

"Shoot, Tap, you know what I mean."

"Yeah. But maybe we need to expand our purpose."

"Like what?"

"Like raising a God-fearing family, putting meat on the table for all them folks back east, and bringing a little civilizin' to this wild country."

"That's easy for you to say, partner. You got the wife and junior on the way."

"You could catch up mighty quick, Odessa."

"Been givin' it some thought."

"You mean Selena?"

"Yeah. What do you think I should do first?"

"Settle up with the Almighty."

"You're serious, ain't ya?"

"Yep. . . . Are you?"

"You figure we'll reach Pine Bluffs tomorrow mornin'?"

"You're changin' the subject, Odessa."

"You got me pinned in a corner, Andrews. I've got to find a loose barn board somewhere."

Tap closed his eyes and thought he felt a slightly cool breeze roll across the prairie.

"You know I'm right, Lorenzo."

"Okay, okay, you're right. Does that make you happy?"

"Yep."

"Now when will we make it to Pine Bluffs?"

"I reckon we'll ride into Pine Bluffs about this time tomorrow mornin'."

"Unless we can catch up with Cabe and Banner first," Lorenzo mumbled.

The second day they rested their horses and themselves more and more often. Sometime in the middle of the night they reached the Union Pacific tracks and headed west toward Pine Bluffs. Tap bypassed the livery and rode straight to his house. Tying the horses up to the fence in the front yard, Andrews pulled his rifle and sauntered to the front door. His boot heels banged on the wooden sidewalk, and his spurs jingled. Down the street a dog barked. To the east, the sky broke into a predawn gray. The slightly bowlegged Lorenzo Odessa followed him, carbine over his shoulder.

Tap banged on the door.

"Who's there?"

The quick reply from right inside the door startled him.

"Angelita?"

"Mr. Andrews?"

"Open the door, little darlin'. It's me."

The thick wooden door swung inward. In the glow of the lantern Angelita stood by the doorway, carrying a shotgun. She dropped the gun and ran to throw her arms around him.

"What's wrong, darlin'? Where's Pepper?"

"They took her!" she sobbed. "They tricked her, and then they took her! And I didn't know what to do! I wanted to go after them. Honest, I did. But Mrs. Andrews said I should stay here with the door locked. And I was scared, really scared and . . . they said you were dying, and I was scared to see you dead."

"Who took her?"

"I don't know!" Angelita sobbed.

"Where's Selena?" Odessa asked.

"They took her, too!"

"Banner and Cabe?" Tap looked back at Odessa. Bending low, he pushed Angelita back an arm's length and looked her in the eyes. "When did this happen and where did they go?"

"Maybe half an hour ago. . . . They said they were goin' to the livery. But if they got horses or a carriage, I don't know where they went!" Angelita began to cry. "I couldn't stop 'em. Honest, I was scared. I tried to take care of Mrs. Andrews like you told me. I'm sorry," Angelita cried.

Tap hugged her again. "It's okay, darlin'. Now you wait here, and me and Odessa will go after the ladies."

"No!" Angelita wailed. "I can't wait here. I have to help. Please!"

Tap wiped the corner of her eyes with his callused thumbs.

Lord, Pepper hasn't had any peace from the day she married me. This is crazy. The one thing in life I want to do most — take good care of her — I'm the biggest failure at.

"Grab that Greener, Angelita, and come on."

She clutched the shotgun and followed Tap and Odessa out the door into the early morning dawn. They had just reached the horses when a deep voice rolled out from the shadows to the left.

"Andrews, I'm here to arrest you!"

Tap raised his rifle in the direction of the voice.

"Don't try it!" came another voice behind them.

"I don't have time for this, Marshal," Tap barked, keeping his rifle raised.

"I got papers."

"And Cabe and Banner are holding my expectant wife and another woman hostage. I've got to find them before they are harmed."

"I don't know anything about that, but —"

"You don't know anything at all," Odessa broke in. "Tap was in Sundance Mountain when Tracker was killed. Me and a dozen others will testify to that."

"Cabe shot Tracker, and now he's threatenin' harm to my wife. Marshal, if you're goin' to use that gun, you better make your play, because I'm goin' to rescue my wife if it's the last thing on earth that I do."

"If I pulled both these triggers, would both barrels fire at once?"

Tap and the marshal glanced back. Angelita had slipped around to the side of the horses and was pointing the shotgun right at the marshal's midsection.

"Just a minute, little girl!" the marshal hollered.

She shoved the shotgun in his midsection. "I'm not a little girl. I'm a young lady."

"Well . . . d-don't point that at me," he stuttered.

Tap and Odessa grabbed the reins of their horses and led the animals across the street.

"Wait! Where are you going? You're under arrest," the marshal cried out.

"Not now. I just don't have time. Maybe we can visit about it over a cup of coffee later."

"Then, eh . . . we'll go with you!" he shouted.

"Well, stay back there out of the way and be quiet. Don't shoot 'em, Angelita. Not unless they do something dumb."

The marshal and his deputy scurried to keep up with Tap and Lorenzo. "How do we know you won't just mount up and try to escape by riding out of town?"

Odessa turned in the street and looked at the lawmen following them. "Why don't you two ride our horses, and we'll walk to the livery?"

Tap gave Lorenzo a look and nodded.

"I'll take the gray; you take the roan." The marshal motioned to his lanky deputy.

The deputy lasted four jumps before the roan deposited him on the hitching rail by the bakery. The thick beam cracked like a toothpick, and the deputy didn't move. The marshal was still clutching the horn with both hands as Roundhouse tore down the alley sideways, rear hooves in the air, head ducked under a full clothesline.

Tap, Odessa, and Angelita raced toward the livery.

"That was a mighty mean trick to play on decent lawmen," Tap chided.

"If they're goin' to stay in the marshalin' business, they better improve their horse-ridin' skills. Maybe we should sell them those two ponies."

Tap ducked down a side street, coming up to the livery from the west side. Squatting down in the dying shadows of night, he surveyed the empty street. Odessa and Angelita hunkered down beside him.

271

"What do we do from here?" Odessa asked. "We don't know if they rode out of town or are hiding in the livery."

"I figure they're in there. They want us, not the women. We might go tearin' out on the prairie and not find them."

"You think they won't harm the women until they take care of us first?"

"That's what I'm hopin'."

"And prayin'?" Odessa quizzed.

Tap nodded. "Angelita, you stay here."

"I want to go in with you," she insisted.

"I need you here. If you hear a lot of gunfire and Cabe or Banner comes out of that building, let 'em have a barrel from back here. That will slow them down and keep you safe. Can you do that for me?"

"I can do it. I won't let you down this time, Mr. Andrews."

"Darlin', you've never let me down in your life." He hugged her. "Come on, Odessa, we've got business across the street."

"Straight at 'em?"

"Yep. I just don't have the time or energy to figure out somethin' fancy."

Both men began walking side by side toward the livery barn. Tap held the rifle at his hip, as did Lorenzo the carbine. Reaching the huge front doors, Tap transferred the rifle to his left hand and pulled his revolver. He motioned for Odessa to swing open the right side door. As he did, Tap dove through the doorway, intending to roll to his knees and come up ready to fire.

Instead, his left knee crashed into the stock of his rifle. The pain forced him to collapse and drop face first into the dirt floor of the livery.

"Just stay right there in the dirt, mister, or your compadre is dead!"

It was a familiar voice.

A woman's voice.

Tap pushed himself up on one elbow.

"Selena?"

"Tap?"

"Tap!" Pepper shouted.

"Pepper darlin', are you all right?" Tap sat up in the dirt and retrieved his dropped rifle.

The two big front doors of the barn swung wide. Daylight revealed the scene inside.

"Miss Selena," Odessa called in, "are you safe?"

"You two weren't worried about us, were you?" Selena called back.

Tap brushed himself off and hobbled with Odessa over to Selena and Pepper in an almost empty stall. The only contents were a roped and tied Colton Banner and Wesley Cabe. Selena held a knife, Pepper a pitchfork.

"For God's sake, Andrews, get this woman away from me!" Banner grumbled. There was blood on the right sleeve of his coat.

Pepper slipped her arms around Tap.

"Are you and little Tap all right, darlin'?" he asked.

"We're fine."

"They didn't hurt you?"

"They didn't get a chance."

"But how . . . I mean, they must have had guns and . . . How did you do that?"

"They made a serious mistake when they tangled with two retired dance-hall girls," Selena explained. She backed away from Banner and strolled over to Odessa, slipping her arm in his.

"Retired?" Lorenzo asked.

"That's up to you, cowboy." Selena winked with a very bruised eye.

Tap pushed his hat back and scratched the back of his neck. "But still I can't figure how you could . . . I mean, Cabe and Banner are the kind who wouldn't hesitate to . . . Here you are, you know, in a womanly way."

"I'm fat!" Pepper managed a slight smile. "But don't ever think ten years in dance halls leaves a girl defenseless. We know how to fight."

"And we don't play by the rules," Selena added, waving the knife at Banner's midsection. "Banner didn't think I'd use my knife. That was a serious mistake."

Pepper waved her arm at the two bound men. "Mr. Cabe let me get too close to a pitchfork. I suppose my motherly condition threw him off guard."

Selena slipped her knife back into the sleeve of her dress. "The first lesson in self-defense in a dance hall is not to bluff. You have to be ready to do whatever you threatened to do."

"When I picked up that pitchfork, I was plan-

274

ning on using it," Pepper agreed. "I guess it's the element of surprise. They don't really think you'll do it."

"I've been worried sick about you for two days," Tap confessed.

"And I've been worried about you most every day for seven months." Pepper slipped her hand into his.

Tap led Pepper to the open barn door. Selena and Lorenzo followed.

"Hey!" Banner called out from the back of the barn. "You can't leave us here! We're bleedin'. We need help!"

Odessa's carbine swung up to his hip as he spun around. "Mister, I've been waitin' for two days to do this," he growled.

"Lorenzo, now's the time to set it aside, partner," Tap hollered. "You know I'm right. God Almighty will give you a new chance, but you have to start somewhere!"

The .44 thundered.

A barn board shattered not more than a foot to the right of Banner's head. The second shot from the hip exploded a board six inches to the left of the trembling man's head.

"Wait!" Banner screamed.

"Did you say somethin' about not wantin' to be left there?" Odessa shouted.

"No!" came a weak, frightened reply.

Lorenzo let his carbine drop to his side as he turned and faced Tap and the others.

"That's a start, Tapadera." He grimaced.

275

"Yep. That's a start."

The four walked out into the light of the Wyoming morning. The sun was just peeking over the eastern prairie horizon. A farm wagon rolled up the street. A rooster crowed. The dog stopped barking. The sky was clear. Pepper could tell it would be another hot, dry day.

"You almost killed me!" a voice shouted from the porch of the closed millinery shop across the street. The marshal and his deputy sat on the steps nursing their bruises. "And you're still under arrest, Andrews."

"If you really want to know who killed Jacob Tracker, you ought to talk to those two tied up in the back stall," Pepper called out. "Cabe admits to killing Tracker."

"Especially if you hold a pitchfork to his neck," Selena added.

The marshal and his deputy hobbled across the street.

"Don't let those two loose," Tap warned. "They're wanted for cattle rustlin' and murder in Texas as well as Wyomin'. If you need to talk to me, I'll be at the house."

Tap tried brushing the dirt off his shirt and then took off his black beaver felt hat. He ran his fingers through his oily hair. He glanced over at Pepper.

"You surely do look purdy in the morning prairie sun, darlin'."

"And you look like a dirty mess. Can we go home now? I'll cook us all some breakfast while you clean up. Angelita will be worried sick."

"Angelita? She's over there. . . . Where did that girl go? She came over with me and Lorenzo." Tap looked up and down the street.

A black carriage pulled by two tall black horses rolled toward the livery.

"There she is!" Pepper pointed to the carriage. "She must have gotten a ride."

"Stack?" Tap stared at the clean-shaven, well-dressed driver of the carriage.

The big man tipped his broad beaver hat. "Miss Selena! What a surprise! Two of my favorite girls."

"Stack," Tap teased, "I hardly recognized you all dressed up like an undertaker."

"Well, Andrews, you look like you've been horsewhipped and dragged through the stockyards. You ain't changed a bit."

"Lowery, what are you doin' in Pine Bluffs? Where's your freight wagon? What's with this boiled white shirt and tie?"

"Ain't you told him about the gold mine?" Stack quizzed.

"I haven't had time," Pepper admitted.

Tap stared at Stack and then at Pepper. "What gold mine?"

"Mr. Lowery happens to own half interest in the largest gold mine in the entire known world," Angelita shouted, and she slipped her hand into Stack's massive right arm.

"He owns what?" Tap choked.

"Don't tell me you haven't mentioned that big

277

Montana ranch either," Stack admonished. "The one I want Tap to run."

"Big . . . Montana . . . ranch?" Tap felt each word slip out of his throat like a large lump of unchewed meat.

"I told you he went down."

"Well, I thought you meant he stumbled."

"He died."

"You mean you rode him to death?"

"No . . . he sort of . . ."

"Sort of what?" Pepper demanded.

"What were you digging, Mr. Andrews?" Angelita interrupted. "Did you bury Brownie?"

"Yep, I did. Most folks don't bury horses in the open like that, but Brownie and me went through a lot together, so I thought it proper. Besides I had to wait for Tom Slaughter to show. He was really grateful to get all sixty-four head back."

"Did they have them rebranded?" Angelita asked.

"Yeah. You see, they took Tom's TS brand and made it into a I8I." Tap squatted down on the porch and wrote in the dust with water from the basin. "Don't ever use *S* in a brand, unless it's a runnin' *S* or a flyin' *S* or something like that."

He stood back up, and Pepper applied some alcohol to his chest. "If I'm not mistaken, you completely changed the subject and are avoiding telling me how Brownie died."

"Now that's a long story, and I'm nearly starved to death. I ate that dinner you put in my saddlebags about 10:30 and haven't had anything but spring water since. Let's eat, and then you can tell me about your day, and I'll tell you about mine."

"Why is it I have a feeling that your day was

31

much more eventful than ours?" Pepper sighed. "Put on your shirt, cowboy. Nobody eats at my table unless they're fully dressed."

Boiled potatoes, beef gravy, stewed tomatoes, fried beef chops, biscuits, and huckleberry preserves covered the small table and the plates almost as completely as the white linen tablecloth. After a leisurely supper, Tap pushed his chair back from the table and drank a third cup of coffee. Angelita gave a detailed description of her confrontation with Matthew Harlow.

"How about you, darlin'? How'd you spend your day?"

"Fat." Pepper spat the word out like a slap.

"You are not fat," Tap protested.

"You are the very man who said I was getting 'fleshed out.' "

"I meant it as a compliment."

"Mr. Andrews, let me tell you something. Calling a woman fleshed out is at no time and under absolutely no conditions ever, ever a compliment!"

"Oh."

"Mr. Andrews has a lot to learn about us women, doesn't he?" Angelita teased.

"Yes, and some days he has more to learn than other days."

"Now, look, you two, before you go hangin' me from a lamppost, make sure you know what I meant when I said that. I realize you don't like all that extra weight and your back's sore, but what I —"

"And my feet are swollen."

"Yes, and —"

"And my legs itch."

"See, what I —"

"And I can't walk two blocks without being winded."

"Yes, but —"

"And I can't sleep at night, and I've lost my appetite —"

"Whoa!" Tap interjected. "Let me finish my thought before I forget it entirely. When I see that belly of yours growin', it means Little Tap is growing. That's good. That's really, really good. When I said you were fleshed out, what I meant was that Little Tap —"

"Or Little Tapette," Angelita corrected.

"Yes. I meant the baby is growing fat. That's a healthy, wonderful thing."

Pepper stared at him for a minute and then turned to Angelita. "What do you think, honey, did he squirm out of it this time?"

Angelita nodded her head. "Yeah, nice squirming, Mr. Andrews."

"Thank you. Do you think it deserves another cup of coffee?"

"I'll get it for you." Angelita jumped up and slipped over to the cookstove.

"Now, Mr. Andrews . . . we are still waiting for a full explanation of how Brownie died," Pepper insisted.

"How about one more biscuit and jam . . . and the three of us sittin' on the front porch? It

33

might be a little cooler out there."

Tap settled at the end of the porch, the back of his chair leaning against the wall of the house as he sipped steaming coffee from an off-white porcelain cup.

Pepper sat next to Tap with needle and thread and a dress draped across her well-rounded stomach.

Angelita slouched in the open doorway, examining each tooth with her fingers.

"What happened to Brownie? How did he die?"

"A bullet in the head," Tap admitted.

"You had to put him down?"

"Actually someone else did the job for me."

"I'm glad someone could help you out. It's tough on you to lose him, isn't it?"

"Me and him went through a lot. Kind of like losin' a good friend."

"That's why you buried him?"

"Yep."

"Other than that, was it pretty much a routine day?" she asked.

"More or less," Tap conceded.

Angelita ran out into the yard as a young man on a sorrel horse rode up toward their house.

"Mr. Andrews!" the young man called.

"Eh . . . young Mr. Parker."

"Butch."

"Okay, Butch. Eh, this is Mrs. Andrews."

Butch tipped his round-crowned hat. "Evenin', ma'am."

34